"You're running scared."

"I'm not scared."

"Oh, yes, you are." Anita stepped forward, pointing a finger at Luke's chest. "You are terrified of me. I know you, Luke, better than you think. You retreat into work and you pretend the world doesn't exist. I'm attracted to you. I'm not going to pretend I'm not, but I'm not foolish enough to have a relationship with you."

"I think I liked it better when you were complimenting my body."

She smiled, then averted her gaze from his. "So, as long as we're clear on this now. No romantic relationship. Just friends."

"Yeah, just friends."

"Good." She nodded, *almost* convincing herself that this was exactly what she'd wanted.

Dear Reader,

Are you headed to the beach this summer? Don't forget to take along your sunblock—and this month's four new heartwarming love stories from Silhouette Romance!

Make Myrna Mackenzie's *The Black Knight's Bride* (SR #1722) the first book in your tote bag. This is the third story in THE BRIDES OF RED ROSE, a miniseries in which classic legends are retold in the voices of today's heroes and heroines. For a single mom fleeing her ex-husband, Red Rose seems like the perfect town—no men! But then she meets a brooding ex-soldier with a heart of gold....

In *Because of Baby* (SR #1723), a pixie becomes so enamored with a single dad and his adorable tot that she just might be willing to sacrifice her days of fun and frivolity for a human life of purpose...and love! Visit a world of magic and enchantment in the latest SOULMATES by Donna Clayton.

Even with the help of family and friends, this widower with a twelve-year-old daughter finds it difficult to think about the future—until a woman from his past moves in down the street. Rest and relaxation wouldn't be complete without the laughter and love in *The Daddy's Promise* (SR #1724) by Shirley Jump.

And while away the last of your long summer day with *Make Me a Match* (SR #1725) by Alice Sharpe. A feisty florist, once burned by love, is supposed to be finding a match for her mother and grandmother...not falling for the town's temporary vet! Matchmaking has never been so much fun.

What could be better than greeting summer with beach reading? Enjoy!

Mavis C. Allen
Associate Senior Editor

Please address questions and book requests to:
Silhouette Reader Service
U.S.: 3010 Walden Ave., P.O. Box 1325, Buffalo, NY 14269
Canadian: P.O. Box 609, Fort Erie, Ont. L2A 5X3

The Daddy's Promise

SHIRLEY JUMP

SILHOUETTE *Romance*®

Published by Silhouette Books

America's Publisher of Contemporary Romance

To my dad, whose love and integrity
taught me that good men do exist. And to my husband,
the best daddy our kids could ever have.

 SILHOUETTE BOOKS

ISBN 0-373-19724-1

THE DADDY'S PROMISE

Copyright © 2004 by Shirley Kawa-Jump

Books by Shirley Jump

Silhouette Romance

The Virgin's Proposal #1641
The Bachelor's Dare #1700
The Daddy's Promise #1724

SHIRLEY JUMP

has been a writer ever since she learned to read. She sold her first article at the age of eleven and from there, became a reporter and finally a freelance writer. However, she always maintained the dream of writing fiction, too. Since then, she has made a full-time career out of writing, dividing her time between articles, nonfiction books and romance. With a husband, two children and a houseful of pets, inspiration abounds in her life, giving her good fodder for writing and a daily workout for her sense of humor.

Dear Reader,

I'm thrilled to be returning to the town of Mercy, Indiana, again and revisiting old friends and neighbors! The Misses, and their dogs, are making a return appearance (back by popular request, after so many readers wrote me and told me how much they loved them in my first two Mercy books), and so is Katie from *The Virgin's Proposal*.

This book was also fun for another reason—I was able to relive all the comical moments from my two pregnancies. Having children was the best gift of my life, but it's also provided me with lots of inspiration for humor, much of which is reflected in *The Daddy's Promise*.

Return to Mercy with me for a few laughs and a few tears.

Chapter One

The mouse won—by default.

If the doorbell hadn't rung, Anita Ricardo was sure she would have won the staring contest with the scrawny rodent. Then she could have chalked up at least one point for herself on this hot, calamity-prone day.

Well, maybe a half point.

The three-note off-key song played again. Not exactly the lyrical melody of the bell back at her apartment in L.A.—the apartment she'd given up to come to Mercy, Indiana, and start a new life.

Unfortunately, right now a new life meant living in a rickety rental house with a rodent for a roommate.

Geez, put that way, her life sounded like the plot of a bad sitcom. Anita got to her feet. She reached for the front door, twisted the knob and pulled. The heavy door refused to budge. For the second time that day, the late-August humidity had swollen it tight to the frame. The first time, she'd been able to use a little elbow grease—little being the operative word for a five-foot-three woman who barely topped a hundred pounds—to wrestle it open.

The doorbell pealed a third time. Anita put both hands on the knob and yanked.

"Just a minute," she yelled. Maybe it was the plumber, here to do something about the sputtering rust that passed for water. Or the electrician the landlord had promised to send over to fix the flickering lights. Or even, please Lord, the telephone company, here to connect her with the outside world.

Anita tugged harder. The door moved a fraction of an inch. She put her weight into it and then—

The knob jerked out of the locking mechanism and right into her hands. Anita stumbled back several steps. She blinked at the brass sphere in her hands.

"Hello?" called a quavering female voice.

"Hang on a minute. I have a bit of a problem here." She tried to slip the knob back into the hole. It refused to connect. Anita bent down, peered through the opening and saw—

A canned ham.

"Um, hello?" Anita said to the pink oval.

The ham moved away, replaced by an eye and part of a wrinkled cheek. "Why hello, dear. Welcome to Mercy." The woman straightened and the ham swung into view again. Fully Cooked, Real Maple Flavor, No Refrigeration Needed. "I'm with the Mercy Welcoming Committee."

"Do you have a screwdriver with you? Maybe a sledgehammer?"

"Did you say *sledgehammer,* dear?"

"Never mind. Let me open the window." The back door, Anita knew from an unsuccessful door-pull match this morning, was likely just as stuck. She straightened, then lifted the sash on the small window, fumbling with the finicky metal screen.

After two good curses and a solid tug, she managed to fling it up. She dipped her head to her knees and crawled out the window and onto the wide wooden porch.

The woman didn't blink at Anita's unconventional entrance. She looked close to eighty years old and wore a bright floral sleeveless dress shaped more like a bell than an hourglass. "Here you go, new neighbor." She thrust the basket into Anita's arms. "I'm Alice Marchand."

Anita staggered a little under the weight of the wicker container. A hand-drawn smiley face dangled from the handle, with the words "Welcome to Our Town" forming the lips. The basket was piled to the brim with a motley collection of foods and household things: a red flashlight emblazoned with Joe's Hardware: Screws You Can Use; two bottles of Pete's Hotter Than Hades Salsa; some calico-topped jars of home-canned food; a Tupperware container of chocolate-chip cookies; and the pièce de résistance, a hand fan from the local funeral home, decorated with Ten Tips for Planning Early for the Afterlife.

The basket took the prize for hokiest gift of the year. And yet it touched some kind of sentimental nerve because, for a brief second, Anita wanted to cry.

Crazy. She was hot, sweaty and tired. Nothing more. A glass of lemonade and a good meal and she'd be back to her regular, optimistic self. "Thank you, Mrs. Marchand."

"Oh, I'm not a missus. Never did find a man I could tolerate." She leaned closer and winked. "Besides, I'm holding out for true love."

Anita chuckled. "The basket is beautiful. Thanks again."

"It's nothing. Just a bit of Indiana hospitality." Miss Marchand bent forward, pointing inside it. "There's some of my neighbor Colleen's homemade orange marmalade in there, and a loaf of bread baked special by the ladies of the Presbyterian Church. Oh, and a coupon for Flo's Cut and Go. Our little beauty shop hasn't been the same since Claire left—that's who rented this house before you. The new girl, Dorene, is trying, bless her heart, but she's just not Claire." Miss Marchand pressed a hand to her gray pouf. "Dorene is mighty stingy with the hairspray. Keep an eye on her with the Aqua Net."

"I'll, ah, keep that in mind." She should invite the woman in for a glass of lemonade, but doubted a senior citizen would be up to a climb through the window. "Would you like something to drink? I can go in and get—"

"Looks like you have your hands full already. And, in a few more months, you'll have them twice as full," she gestured toward Anita's stomach.

Anita glanced down at her legging shorts and oversize T-shirt. She'd just hit the seventh month of her pregnancy and had outgrown most of her regular clothes but hadn't yet bought many maternity clothes. Stretchy outfits and sundresses were comfortable and the easiest on her tight budget. "How did you know I'm pregnant?"

"Old lady's intuition. Not to mention, the little clues sitting in the porch swing." She smiled, gesturing toward the pregnancy guide Anita had left out there earlier that morning. Beside it sat two pairs of half-crocheted baby booties, one in pink and one in blue.

"Oh, those! I—"

Miss Marchand waved a hand in dismissal. "No need to explain. It's nice to see someone young making something by hand," she said. "You have a nice day. Oh, and if you need any work done or help with anything, call John Dole. His number's in there. Now that he's retired, he works part-time as a handyman. Nicest man you'd ever want to meet, and with the smartest sons you've ever seen. I should know. They all passed my biology class with flying colors. Why, Claire even married one of them." Miss Marchand smiled. "She always was a bright girl."

"Did you say John *Dole?*" Anita's breath lodged in her throat. "Does he have a son named Luke?"

Miss Marchand nodded. "Along with Mark and Nate and Katie. Quite the family, the Doles. If you ever get to meet any of them, you'll love them to pieces."

"I already have." In that instant, Anita saw Luke's face again, half in shadow in his darkened office. That kiss—no, not a kiss, more an eruption of hot, molten desire. One kiss, nothing more, but it had been enough to scare Luke away and to tip Anita's perfect, planned-out world off-kilter. "Is he...is he living in town now?"

Miss Marchand smiled and her silvery blue eyes perked up. "Why, yes he is, dear. He was working at the steel mill, but now he's got a business at home. He lives just a couple blocks down, too. It's the little white house on Cherry Street. You should stop over and say hello. If you're old friends and all." The sentence came out with a lilt at the end, more question than declaration.

"Actually, he's the reason I'm here."

"Oh?" Miss Marchand gave Anita's swollen belly an obvious glance.

"Oh, no, this isn't his baby." She laughed. "When I knew him in California, he raved so much about Mercy, he made it sound like paradise. At least, compared to L.A. That's why we're here." She pressed a hand to her abdomen.

"Does he know you're here?"

"No, I...well, I haven't had a chance to tell him." Seeing Luke wasn't part of her plan. Men in general weren't part of her plan. All Anita cared about was settling in a nice place, where her baby could grow up happy and healthy, with neighbors who wrapped around their lives like a well-worn quilt. Mercy, with its quaint streets and quiet neighborhoods, seemed perfect so far.

"Well, I wouldn't worry about that." The old woman winked. "News spreads faster than chicken pox here. I'm sure Luke will be dropping in to see you soon."

Anita doubted that, but left those words unsaid. "This basket looks great. I really appreciate the welcome."

Miss Marchand wasn't dissuaded by a change of topic. "If you ever want to talk to Luke, just call John. Luke's there, staying with his folks for a bit. That young man's been through an awful time." She tugged on a leather strap and a little dachshund Anita hadn't noticed before scrambled to her feet, wagging her tail, clearly anxious to be on her way again. When Miss Marchand reached the sidewalk, the dachshund hopped into a little red wagon, obviously the basket's conveyance. "The number's right behind the ham!"

Miss Marchand toodled a wave, then picked up the wagon's handle and set off down the sidewalk. Anita stayed on the porch, hugging the basket to her chest.

In L.A., no one would have done something so nice. Her neighbors had never introduced themselves to her or taken the time to give her the phone number of a handyman. It proved to her once again that she had made the right choice for her and her baby.

The hokier the better, that was her motto from here on out. Hokey was good for raising a family.

A plaintive squeak-squeak sounded behind her. The mouse sat on the windowsill, nose twitching, watching her. He blinked several times, raised his teeny snout in the air, sniffing.

"Don't get any ideas," Anita told him. "I'm not sharing."

The mouse lowered his head, stretched his body toward her. When he did, he looked skinny and deprived. Lonely.

Anita glanced inside the basket and spotted a package of wheat crackers. "Oh, all right. But just one."

She withdrew a cracker from the package and tossed it on the flaking paint of the porch floor. The mouse scrambled down and dove for the cracker. Anita thrust the basket through the window, clambered in after it and shut the screen.

There. She might not have any hot water. Or a front door she could open. Or reliable electricity. But she had managed to outsmart one wily mouse.

Surely, that was a sign her life was on the upswing. If not, she had a flashlight, a hand fan and plenty of cookies to tide her over.

Luke Dole had been pacing the carpet in his daughter's bedroom for the past twenty minutes, mashing an even path in the beige plush. He ran through a mental list of places where Emily could be for the hundredth time and got nowhere. Nothing.

She'd taken off right after school. When the principal called five minutes later to announce Emily's latest act of defiance and impending suspension—only one week into the new school year—Luke knew why his daughter had disappeared.

Now it was ten-thirty, an hour and a half past Emily's curfew, and he had no idea where she could be. He'd already gone out looking once and come up empty. He'd returned home, hoping to find her here, but her bed was still made, her sandals missing from their place by the door. Images of serial killers, rave parties and fiery car wrecks ran through his mind like a horror slide show.

"Reminds me of when I used to wait up for you and your brother."

His father's voice made Luke jump. He spun around and saw John Dole standing in the doorway, wrapped in a navy terry-cloth robe, holding a glass of water.

"Dad! I didn't hear you get up."

"Well, I heard you. Sounds like a herd of elephants in here." John crossed and took a seat on the edge of Emily's bed. The worn Barbie comforter seemed too girlie for tall, broad John. "I'm sure she's fine, Luke. Just testing some boundaries."

"Yeah, well those boundaries are an hour and a half late. Where could she be?" He began pacing again. "I should call the police."

"Mercy isn't L.A., Luke. Don't you remember what it was like to be twelve, going on thirty? You and Mark were a handful then. Always taking off, building forts, chasing frogs, cornering poor Miss Tanner's dog and painting it purple."

Luke laughed. "I think Miss Tanner's still mad at us for that one."

"That dog of hers was a pain in the neck anyway. Barked at gnats, for God's sake." John sipped, then placed the glass on Emily's white wicker nightstand. When she'd been seven, Emily had loved this bedroom set, right down to the Barbie-and-Ken pillowcase. But now, it seemed to be one more thing for them to argue about. Luke hated that she was outgrowing the memories he and Mary had worked so hard to build.

His father rose, put a hand on his shoulder. "Em's

going through a tough time. Losing her mother just when she needed her most.''

"I lost Mary, too, Dad. I don't know how to do this. I don't know how to be two parents at once." He'd carried this load alone for almost two years, and he'd dropped it more than once. "I keep screwing it up."

"You and she have a few things to work out, that's all. It'll be all right."

Luke had heard those words so many times. From the psychiatrist he'd hired for Emily after Mary died, from the teachers and principals who had thrown up their hands after unsuccessfully trying to reverse Emily's failing grades and continued rule breaking, from the neighbors who thought they were doing the right thing by bringing over hot dishes and well-worn platitudes. He'd moved back home, hoping his parents could help him break through the brick wall she'd put up.

Maybe he wasn't the right man to raise Emily. Maybe another man would have—

That thought damn near broke his heart in two. He hung his head. Thick emotion clogged his throat, strangling his vocal cords. "*When*, Dad? When is it ever going to be right again?"

John's eyes shimmered. "I wish I had that answer for you." He gripped Luke tight for a moment. "Go find Emily. Talk to her. I've never seen two people who needed each other more."

How true that was. Each of them was all the other had left. And yet, they kept pushing each other away as if they were fighting over the last lifeboat on a sinking ship.

Luke gave his father a quick, one-armed hug, then headed for the door.

Once again, he drove up and down the streets of Mercy. It was a small town, barely more than six thousand in population, so there wasn't much area to cover. For half an hour, he saw nothing but the occasional loose dog. And then, on the corner of Lincoln and Lewis, he saw a familiar figure with fuchsia hair and a bright orange T-shirt climbing in the window of a house.

Claire Richards used to live there, until she'd married Luke's twin brother, Mark, and they'd moved to California. Renters were few and far between in Mercy, and the home had fallen into disrepair and become a teen party hangout over the last twelve months. His mother had mentioned something about a new person moving in, but Luke had barely caught the comment and didn't remember if his mother had said there was a tenant already in residence or soon to be.

The house was dark, looked empty. Emily would see it as the perfect hiding place.

Luke parked his Chevy in front of the neighbor's house. He snuck down the drive, around to the back of Claire's, then hoisted himself into the window Emily had disappeared through.

Anita bolted upright in bed. The sound she'd heard coming from the next bedroom—the one she'd started setting up as an office—hadn't come from a mouse.

Unless the mouse had invited a few million friends over for a canned-ham-and-marmalade party.

Her heart hammered in her chest. Images of her certain demise flashed through her mind: the coroner shaking his head at the woefully unprepared corpse, the headline decrying the loss of the newest Mercy resident and all that wasted food from the Welcoming Committee.

Anita took a deep breath, clearing her head.

A weapon. She needed a weapon. In the half light of the moon through the curtainless windows she didn't see anything remotely lethal, unless she counted one pair of red spike heels.

Then, in the corner, a box labeled "Kitchen," left there when she got too tired to move anything else. Eureka. She prayed for a rolling pin, maybe even that cast-iron waffle maker she'd never used but felt compelled to tote across the country, in case she ever had a hankering for homemade Belgians.

Anita crept out of bed, snuck over to the box and pried open the cardboard lid. From the other room, a scuffling sound. She held her breath, praying Jack the Ripper wasn't about to lunge through the door and show off his superior surgical skills.

She pulled out the first thing her hand lighted on. A Teflon skillet. Twelve inches of coated aluminum, with a wooden handle. Not a heck of a lot more lethal than the stilettos, but easier to wield and requiring far less accuracy.

Anita got to her feet, steadying her stomach with her hand when a wave of nausea threatened to undo her. She crept out of her room, down the short hall and toward the next doorway. Like a SWAT-team leader, she plastered herself to the wall, peeking around the corner, pan at the ready above her head.

At first, she didn't see much but then, a flash at the window.

A man was on the window ledge, heaving himself into the room. A large man. Son of Sam size. Anita slithered around the doorway, pressed herself to the wall and crept barefoot around the perimeter of the room.

He didn't notice her. He was too busy huffing and puffing his way through a B and E. He paused, his hands propped on the sill. Anita reached him and before she could think about what she was about to do, she raised the pan, then swung it down as hard as she could. Her muscles—or maybe her conscience—flickered at the last second, turning her crushing blow into nothing more than a cornflake-crunching glance.

The man let out an oomph, lifted his hands to ward off future attacks and promptly fell forward, landing face first with a thud on the wood floor.

Anita raised the pan, ready to strike again. She hesitated.

There was a man on her floor. A large man. If she knocked him out, how would she ever get him out the door? That is, if she could even *open* the door. She could call the police, but her phone still wasn't hooked up and for all she knew, Mercy, being such a small town, didn't have a full-time police department, just some local yokels who probably took the law into their own hands after work. Maybe she should get the stilettos. Threaten him with the pointy end and make him crawl out.

But first, she'd be smart. Force him to fix that door. And maybe move the kitchen table to the other side of the room. Every once in a while, her choice to be manless presented a few logistical problems.

Anita hoisted the pan higher. If worse came to worse, she could tie him up with the useless telephone line and leave him for the mouse.

"Hey! That's my dad!" A female voice shrieked behind her. "Don't hit him!" Before Anita could react, the pan was yanked out of her hand by a girl not much bigger than her.

The man on the floor groaned. He put a hand to his head and rolled over. "Who are you and what are you doing in Claire's—" He leaned forward, blinking. *"Anita?"*

She knew that voice. And that face. It couldn't be him. Absolutely, positively could not be him. She could almost hear Rod Serling humming "Do-do, do-do…" in her ear.

The man on her floor wasn't a bungled burglar. He was…

"Luke?"

"Dad! Don't talk to her. She's crazy. Not to mention, she tried to kill you." The girl dropped the pan on the floor and crossed to her father. Anita remembered meeting his daughter—Emily was her name—a couple of times when the girl had still worn pigtails. Now she hovered over Luke, not touching him, feigning indifference, but it was clear she was concerned. "Are you, like, okay?"

"I'm fine." Luke got to his feet, brushing off his pants as he did. He turned to Anita, his eyes and mouth wide with shock. "If that's how you say hello, I'd hate to see you say goodbye."

Chapter Two

Luke didn't bother to contain his surprise at seeing Anita in Mercy. It had been at least fifteen months since he'd seen her, and now she was living three blocks from him? What puzzle piece had he missed? "What are you doing here?"

"I live here."

"Why?"

"Hey, you're the one breaking and entering." Anita bent to retrieve the skillet. When she did, her oversize nightshirt rode up, exposing long, creamy legs. The moonlight streaming through the window illuminated her face with a soft glow. "Since I'm holding the Teflon, I'll ask the questions. Why are you climbing through my office window?"

"I was looking for Emily, who didn't come home when she was supposed to." He shot his pink-haired daughter the parental evil eye. She shrugged and got busy drawing a circle on the floor with her toe. "I saw her climbing into your house and went in after her."

"I was just looking for a place to crash," Emily muttered.

"You were avoiding punishment," Luke said. "For that…" He gestured, wordless, at her neon-dyed head.

Emily let out a chuff of disgust, crossed her arms over her chest. "I hate my life."

Anger boiled up inside of Luke. "Emily Anne, get in the car right now. You're grounded for the next three hundred years."

Emily parked her fists on her hips. "You can't make me."

Luke half expected steam to come pouring out of his ears. *"Emily."*

Anita stepped forward and laid the pan on a box. She lifted her hand, as if she was about to touch Luke, then withdrew at the last second. A ripple of disappointment ran through him.

Maybe that bump on the head had knocked a couple of screws loose.

"Let me get an ice pack for your head," she said. "And lemonade for everyone. Then we can all cool down and start over."

Just as she had so many times before when she'd been the marketing consultant for his and Mark's software company, Anita defused the situation with a few quiet words. They'd brought her in for the launch of the company six years ago, but she'd stayed even when they couldn't pay her anymore. She'd stayed because she had been a friend.

And for a very brief moment, much more than that for Luke. But then…

He pushed those thoughts away. He wasn't going to go there, not now, not later. His priority, now more than ever, was Emily. Women, and this woman in particular, didn't figure into that equation.

Exactly what he'd told Anita, and himself, nearly a year and a half ago. Looking at her now, he needed a refresher course.

Why was she living in Mercy? Why here out of all the thousands of towns in the country? Was she here to rekindle things with him? Or worse, to confront him about the callous way he'd broken off their relationship? He decided not to ask—just in case the answer was one his daughter shouldn't hear.

His head throbbed where the pan had connected with his skull. "You pack a decent wallop." He probed the spot gingerly.

Anita turned, smiled. "I went easy on you, too." Maybe it was just the intimacy of the hallway or the soft glow of the moon on her features, but her smile caused a deep twisting in his gut that he hadn't felt in a long time.

Anita was here. In his life again. A thousand different emotions, like a shower of fireworks, erupted in his gut.

He should leave now, before he started traveling down a path he knew he shouldn't take. But his feet kept moving forward, propelling him with a will of their own.

The house was small and they entered the dark

kitchen a second later. He reached past Anita and pulled the chain attached to the ceiling-fan light.

"I wouldn't do that if I were you," Anita said, reaching for his hand at the same time. Their palms collided. Luke jerked back when an almost electric jolt coursed through him, harder and faster than the Teflon blow. The light burst on, making everyone blink.

"It seems to be working fine." The circular light fixture hanging from the center of the ceiling glowed brightly…maybe a bit too brightly. Then there was a sizzle and a hiss, followed by a loud pop. A shower of sparks and shattered bulb glass rained over them and the small wooden kitchen table.

The room was thrust into darkness again.

"Way to go, Dad," Emily said.

Anita sighed and brushed the glass off her shoulders and hair. "What is it with men? Why do they always think they know everything?"

"Because we do." Luke chuckled. "Or at least, we like to pretend we do. Makes up for our natural insecurity."

Anita's light laughter echoed in the quiet. "This coming from the same guy who always insisted he knew where he was going, even when he was heading for Oregon instead of San Francisco?"

In the dark, her teasing seemed more intimate, almost like a joke between longtime lovers. He remembered that car ride with her. Two glorious hours, spent lost and wandering up and down the California coastline. Well, he'd really only been lost half the time. He'd never admitted that to her, though.

Luke cleared his throat. "Well. Do you have a candle or something?"

"Right here." Anita flared a match and lit a candle that sat on the table. She blew the match out, then crossed the kitchen to get a small broom and dustpan.

In the amber candlelight, she looked even more beautiful, glowing almost, than the last time he'd seen her. He'd always thought the name Anita fit her— lyrical and tough, all at the same time.

Her hair was shorter now. It was still the same shade of deep rich brown, reflecting the light in shimmers of cranberry. Eighteen months ago, her hair had reached past her shoulders, cascading in waves that curled at the ends. Now the tendrils teased around her neck, emphasizing her delicate features like a custom frame.

Here she was, standing in his brother's wife's old house.

Why? Had she sought him out? Come to finish what had been left undone between them? And why did that thought both terrify and unnerve him?

For a moment, he pictured finishing what they'd started back in California. But one glance at his daughter, sitting sullenly in a kitchen chair, drumming her fingers on the table, reminded him where his priorities lay.

"Lemonade? Or iced tea?" Anita gestured toward a cooler.

Her chocolate eyes met his, and the spark of electricity jolted through him again. "Uh…we need to get home. Thanks, but…we need to get home."

She smiled. "You said that already."

He couldn't have acted more like a blubbering idiot if he'd tried. For once, he longed to have just a pinch of the charm his twin had. A few suave words that could get him out of Anita's house with his ego intact.

Instead, he mumbled something about it being late, grabbed a protesting Emily by the hand and left by the back door before he humiliated himself further.

"How does house arrest until you're eighteen sound?" Luke asked Emily. His anger at her disappearance, and his pan bashing, returned full force.

It was also far easier to focus on lecturing Emily than to think about why Anita was here. And why her presence had upset his life's applecart with the force of a small tidal wave.

"We could get you one of those electronic monitors on your ankle so you can't stray more than fifty yards from the front porch. Because that's as far as you're going for the next week. *If* I ever let you out of your room again."

No answer. Emily crossed her arms in front of her chest and stared out the window of the car, practicing for Statue of the Year.

His daughter hadn't said more than three words to him in so long, he'd begun to wonder if she was working toward a career in mime.

"I talked to the principal at school today." No response. "The school year started a week ago and already you're on out-of-school suspension until Friday for breaking the dress-code rules. Again. You knew this would happen. What were you thinking when you put that stuff in your hair?"

He glanced to his right and saw Emily's profile, so like her mother's. Underneath the neon pink, she had Mary's hair color and eyes, the same classic blond and blue-eyed beauty. Despite all that had gone wrong—and all the mistakes he had made and could not undo—Luke loved Emily. He had never doubted his feelings for her. Some days, that was all that kept him at it, a miner trying like hell to break down the wall that stood between him and his daughter.

He reached out a hand to touch her, then withdrew, knowing she'd only pull further away.

They reached the driveway of his parents' house. Before he could bring the sedan to a halt, Emily threw open her door and dashed into the house. Luke sighed, put the car in Park and followed after her, feeling one hundred, not thirty.

When had his daughter become this angry preteen who had about as much fondness for her father as she did for an extra helping of turnips?

What happened to the kid who used to climb all over him, begging Daddy to play one more game before bed? The same little girl who'd ended each night with butterfly kisses against his cheek and bear-tight hugs that made her squeak?

Where was his life? Not the one he used to have, but the one he'd dreamed of having when Emily had been born?

Luke shook his head, forcing himself to stop dwelling on the past. There was a future for him, and for Emily, he knew it.

He just didn't know where it was...or how to reach it.

* * *

On Monday morning, Anita was sitting at her kitchen table, spreading bitter orange marmalade on the bread from the Welcoming Committee basket.

Mental note—never eat anything cooked by Colleen Tanner again. Either the woman had the cooking skills of a chimpanzee or she'd underdone the sugar measurement. The marmalade tasted like orange peel mixed with cement dust.

Anita pinched her nose and choked down another bite. Besides the canned ham, she didn't have much else to eat, at least not until her paycheck came in the mail. She'd used up most of her savings to move here, pay for first, last and security and keep her gas tank filled for the cross-country drive with the rented U-Haul carrying all her furniture attached to the back.

The Honda had needed a lot of coaxing to make it the last couple hundred miles. Anita had begged the little car not to give up the ghost until she reached Mercy, throwing in a promise of a thorough tune-up and lube job as soon as she got paid again.

Any day now, though, the freelance writing job she'd started right before she left would kick in, with payment for all the articles she'd written prior to moving. It was a hefty check, enough to pay her bills, fill the refrigerator—should the electricity ever start working—and give her money to expand her maternity wardrobe.

And, she couldn't forget the booties.

Anita's friend Gena had raved about the first two pairs Anita had made and she'd insisted on trying them in her L.A. boutique. When the crocheted baby socks sold out in a single day, Gena had ordered another fifty pairs, as fast as Anita's crochet hook could create them. Between moving and unpacking, she hadn't had much time. Next week, she'd be able to complete a few pairs and get them out to Gena. Who would have thought a hobby taught to her by her mother could have the potential for becoming a nice side business?

Despite the fact that she had no running water and a rodent in residence, Anita remained optimistic. The glass was half full, and the baby was on his or her way. Plenty to be excited about, even more to look forward to.

The weather report called for a cooling rain. The landlord had promised to send over an electrician first thing. The phone company had assured her there'd be a working line connected to the house sometime between the hours of eight and five. By the end of today, she'd have almost everything she needed.

Anita pressed a hand to her belly. *Things are looking up, kiddo.*

Ever since she'd walked into the Do-It-Yourself-Babies Sperm Bank in L.A., she'd known she was on the right course. All her life, Anita had wanted only one thing—a family. She wasn't going to wait around for true love, if it even existed, to fall into her life and give her the family she wanted. Especially not once Nicholas made it clear that he had no interest in children, despite the diamond he had placed on her finger. Their brief, tempestuous relationship had begun at the end of last summer and been over before winter's gray days left. She'd given the ring back and decided this was one thing she could do on her own. No man necessary.

After the test came back positive, she'd given her notice at the marketing company and at her apartment building, then set out to build a new life for herself and her child. When she was little, her mother had spoken fondly of some small town in Indiana where she'd grown up. In the years since her mother had died she'd forgotten the name, but the flavor of the memory had stayed.

Her mother's stories made the town sound like the perfect place to settle down when she had a child of her own. Mercy, Indiana, was the closest thing Anita knew of to the town her mother had described. After so many years of feeling disconnected, Anita hoped Mercy would provide the answer she was seeking.

The mail truck pulled up in front of her house and slid a pile of letters into the battered aluminum box. Anita crossed into the family room, reached for the front door handle, realized it was still missing in action, and opted for the window.

From the thickness of the stack in the box, Anita figured her mail from L.A. had finally managed to catch up with her. She flipped through the envelopes as she climbed back through the window and into the house.

She tossed the bills to one side of the kitchen table, along with a bunch of junk mail. At the bottom of the pile was a thin envelope she almost missed. Anita tore into it.

The letter from her editor at the magazine started out friendly enough, then disintegrated into bad news.

"Budget cuts... We regret to inform you... Wonderful writing...no further need for your services... Wish you luck elsewhere."

The job she'd counted on was gone. Eliminated with a single sheet of paper and a thirty-seven cent stamp.

Attached to the letter was a check, for only forty percent of what she'd expected. The kill fee, which editors offered when they couldn't use work they'd contracted to buy, wasn't nearly enough.

When she'd landed that job, she'd thought it had been wonderful luck. Here was her chance to build a work-from-home career that would let her be with the baby and still earn a living. She'd figured between the booties business and the savings from living in Mercy instead of L.A., she'd come out ahead.

But now it looked as if she'd fallen behind.

Outside, thunder rumbled. A minute later, the skies let loose. Rain pounded down, slapping against the pavement with determination. In the right-hand corner of the kitchen, a steady drip-drip-drip began. Anita grabbed a three-quart pot and put it under the leak.

The water started dripping a symphony throughout the house. By the time she was done, she'd used five pots, two mixing bowls and all six of her glasses to catch the interior rainstorm.

Add one roofer to the list.

The mouse skittered across the floor, nose twitching, tail flicking. He glanced up at the kitchen table, then scurried around the chairs. He paused, curved his head up to look at her and sniffed twice.

"You're pitiful when you beg." Anita laid a crust

of bread, topped with some of the horrendous marmalade, on the floor. The mouse tiptoed up to it, took one sniff and dived headfirst into his little mouse hole in the kitchen wall.

She laughed. "I don't blame you. Give me a few days and we'll be dining on steak. Well, at least chicken. I'll come up with something."

Things, after all, could be worse. She had a canned ham. Crackers. And marmalade she could use as putty. Not exactly the best choices from the four food groups, but she wouldn't starve.

Anita grabbed her laptop and headed for her Honda. She'd get to the library, hook up to the Internet and scour the Web until she landed another freelance job. Then tonight she'd work like a little elf, crocheting until her fingers fell off.

She had credentials, clips, experience. She'd be fine.

There. A plan. Already she felt better. The rain sputtered against the Honda. Anita turned the key in the ignition.

Click, click, click. Then, nothing.

"Come on, baby." She pressed on the gas pedal, turned the key again and prayed.

This time, the car didn't even bother to click. Nothing but silence.

She climbed out of the vehicle, shut the door and popped the hood. Everything looked normal. The same jumble of wires and metal that had been there for the past six years.

No job. No car. No money. Even Anita had to admit she was facing a problem she didn't have a ready solution for.

She didn't know anyone yet in town, except for Miss Marchand, whom she doubted would be very mechanical. Maybe she could catch a ride downtown in the little red wagon.

There's always Luke, her mind reminded her. Nope, she wasn't going to call on him for help. Relying on Luke would be opening doors best left shut.

Or…there was his father, the part-time handyman. Maybe his skills included giving CPR to dead Hondas. She slung her laptop over her shoulder, grabbed an umbrella out of the hall closet, left a note for the electrician to go in through the back door—if he wanted to steal some unpacked boxes, more power to him—and then set out for Cherry Street in her sandals and sundress.

Mercy was a small town and within fifteen minutes, Anita had found it. The third house down was a white ranch with a hand-painted sign in the shape of a happy yellow daisy announcing, "The Doles Welcome You."

She walked up the brick path, hesitating before she rang the bell. She told herself she didn't care if Luke was the one on the other side of the door.

And yet, if that was true, the voice in the back of her mind asked, then why had she moved within three blocks of the only man she'd ever really trusted? Why did she care so much about the way his shoulders seemed to sag, the dark circles beneath his eyes and the way he looked at his daughter as if he was missing a piece of his soul?

Luke Dole didn't fit into her plans for the future. Heck, he'd barely fit through her window.

He was the exact kind of man she didn't need—a workaholic who spent more time at the office than living his life. And Anita wasn't the kind of woman who relied on other people. Life had taught her that people left her, just when she needed them most. She was just fine on her own, thank you very much.

Nope, she wasn't about to let Luke Dole in through the front door—of the house or of her heart. Not again.

Chapter Three

The doorbell chimed "Hail, Hail, the Gang's All Here," the happy song pealing through the rooms, carrying into the small office space Luke had created in the alcove off the kitchen.

He stopped working on the program he was designing for the newest client Mark had landed for their software business, created last year after Mark's brilliant brainstorm, and got to his feet. He stretched, feeling the hours in the chair kinking in his back. Working at home for the past year had been nice, and convenient for keeping an eye on Emily, but at the end of the day, Luke missed the comfortable leather chair he'd had in the California office. An early-American maple kitchen chair just didn't cut it—unless he had the spine of a rhino.

Before he could get to the door, Emily flounced into the kitchen. "I'm going out." She grabbed her book bag off the counter and slung it over her shoul-

der. She'd changed into a shirt that said Angel across
the front, with a little silver halo. Luke decided it was
best not to comment on the irony of her outfit.

"You're grounded, maybe for the rest of your natural life. Remember?"

"But, *Dad.*"

The doorbell chimed again. Luke crossed to the
door, ignoring the mutiny sparking in Emily's eyes.
"I said no—" he began as he opened the door. The
sentence died in his throat.

Anita. Standing on his front porch, looking wet and
tired and more beautiful than anything he'd seen in a
long time. Luke gulped and, for a minute, forgot
where he was.

His gaze traveled over her heart-shaped face, past
the delicate earlobes, down the long elegant curve of
her neck, over the inviting swell of her breasts, strain-
ing against the sunflower-yellow dress.

He stopped when he noticed the visible bulge at
her waist.

Anita was pregnant?

His gaze flickered to her left hand. Empty.

And unmarried?

He caught his jaw before it dropped to the floor.
But…but…

Try as he might, he couldn't get his mind around
the thought of Anita pregnant and alone.

"I'm not a piece of art, you know," Anita said,
her voice light.

Luke jerked his attention back to Anita's face.
"Sorry. It's been a tough morning." He opened the
door wider. "Come in."

She took a step inside, pausing in the entry hall. "Actually, I was looking for your father."

"My father?"

"My car died. Miss Marchand said your dad was a handyman of sorts, which is just what I need right now. I have no idea what's wrong with the car. I'm not very engine literate." She laughed. "Okay, not at all. I don't think I could tell a dipstick from a piston."

He chuckled, leaning against the wall. "Remind me never to let you work on my Chevy."

She held up a palm. "Scouts' Honor. I'll stay far away."

He smirked. "When were you a Girl Scout?"

"Never." Anita laughed. "Hey, but in a pinch, I can sell you a box of cookies and start a fire with a good set of matches."

Luke glanced down at her and wanted to ask about the obvious pregnancy, but couldn't think of a tactful way to do it. So he bumbled along with the only question he could come up with. "There isn't anyone with you who knows about cars?"

"I live alone." She didn't elaborate.

Luke should have realized that last night. There'd been one dish in the sink, one glass on the countertop. "That must be hard," he said.

"Not really." She smiled, but it was clear she wasn't going to talk about the lack of a man in her life. "I do quite well as a hermit. Except when it comes to Home and Auto Maintenance 101. Then I could use a team of experts, especially with *that* rental house."

"It didn't look too bad last night. Well, except for the light in the kitchen."

She laughed. "It all looks good in the dark. Let's see," she began, ticking off the items on her fingers, "my front door is stuck. The roof leaks, the water is the color of coffee, the telephone doesn't work and oh, there's this mouse—"

"Whoa!" He held up his hands. "I think you win the Worst Day Award. My dad won't be back for a few hours, so why don't you come into the kitchen, have a cup of coffee." He grinned. "We'll work on the rest later." He reached out and took her hand, intending only to lead her into the kitchen. Heat flared between them when he touched her, as if he'd set off a two-alarm fire without meaning to. Luke stepped back, releasing Anita's palm, and stuffed his hands into his pockets, then led the way down the hall. "I, ah, guess a lot has happened to you since the last time I saw—" he began, but was cut off by his daughter.

"*Dad,* I need to go to the library. I have a report due on Friday." Emily was leaning against the kitchen counter, arms crossed, toe tapping against the vinyl.

Now she was interested in schoolwork. Luke figured it was more a means of escape than scholarly intent. "No."

She dropped into a chair and dumped her book bag on the floor. "Fine. I'll just fail history then."

Luke sighed. So much for the light mood he'd slipped into when Anita had arrived. "You can look up the information you need in the encyclopedias Grandma has in the den."

She rolled her eyes. "I need current stuff. Like from this year, not the Stone Age."

"You have to stay here, Emily. You broke the rules and being grounded is part of your punishment."

She kicked at her bag. "So when I fail, can I blame you?"

"Blame yourself. If you hadn't—"

"I have my laptop with me," Anita interrupted, patting the black bag on her shoulder. "I was on my way to the library to do some work because my phone line hasn't been connected yet. I could help Emily look up some information from here."

Emily stuck out her chin, pouting. She huffed, then sighed. "That sounds okay," she conceded.

Luke threw up his hands. "I don't know why I didn't think of that. I'm a software developer, for Pete's sake. You'd think I'd make the computer connection."

"You've had a lot on your mind lately." Anita's voice was soft, understanding. She stepped closer to him, lowering her tone. "Let me help her. Maybe someone other than Dad can get through easier." She cast a smile at him, one that seemed to say she understood preteens. A small measure of calm rippled through him.

"Okay." He smiled. "When we worked together on that launch project two summers ago, you weren't such a bad taskmaster."

"Gee, flatter a girl." She laughed.

"I didn't mean—"

"I know." She smiled again, then brushed past him on her way to the kitchen table, leaving the faint scent of jasmine in her wake. The lusty fragrance jetted Luke's mind back to that night eighteen months ago, to the memory of her in his arms, her body entwined with his, her lips—

What the hell was he doing? The last thing he needed to do was take a trip down Memory Lane right now.

Luke let out a deep breath, regaining control of his senses and his racing pulse. Emily was his priority. His life could be put on hold. Hers was just beginning and she didn't need a father who was distracted by a new relationship. Besides Anita clearly had other priorities.

That thought set off a strange plummeting feeling in his gut. Anita was entitled to a life, a man. He shouldn't be bothered one iota about her personal life.

But he was. More than he wanted to admit.

Anita sat at the table, then opened a black case that held a slightly outdated laptop. Luke could see from the brand name and model that she'd selected the best. She had good taste in technology, something he respected.

"I'm Anita," she said, turning to Emily and sticking out her hand. "I don't think you remember me, and we didn't exactly have a proper introduction last night. The last time I saw you, you were ten and visiting your dad's office after school."

Emily hesitated. "Nice to meet you again." As if the politeness had cost her, she quickly scrambled to get her books out of the backpack.

Anita unraveled a telephone line that was tucked inside her bag and inserted one end into the computer.

"Do you mind if we tie up the phone lines for a minute?"

Luke barely heard the question. He was too busy watching her deftly connect the power cord, flip up the top and start the laptop.

Anita had long, delicate fingers, more fitting for a concert pianist than a marketing consultant. She had a graceful ease about her appearance, as if she felt comfortable anywhere. And when she was happy, her lips curved into a welcoming smile that slid through Luke like silk.

She shifted in her chair and her skirt crept up, exposing another three inches of leg. Who'd have thought that such a tiny measurement could get his heart sprinting like a runner at the start of a race?

"Luke? Can I use the phone line?" Anita's question brought him back to reality.

"Oh. Yeah." He cleared his throat. "Sure." He took the cord and plugged it into the phone jack.

"Thanks." Anita turned back to her computer, clicking with the mouse until the browser program was open and dialing up to the Internet.

Emily scowled and dropped her chin into her hands. "I hate history."

"Those who don't study it are doomed to repeat it, you know," Anita said.

"The chances of me starting the next world war are about the same as me ending up on tour with Mandy Moore."

Anita laughed. "You and me both. I can't sing at all. But I love to pretend I can, with a hairbrush, a mirror and a cranked stereo."

Emily face turned a slight shade of pink. "Me, too," she said quietly. "I thought only kids did that kind of thing."

Anita leaned close and lowered her voice. "Just between you and me, I've had a hard time giving up the dream of being the next Shania Twain."

Emily smiled. Almost laughed.

"I remember seeing you get pretty cozy with a karaoke machine once," Luke said. Anita's voice, clear and strong. Her face, lively, animated, laughing. It had been some client's party Mark and Anita had insisted he go to, two months after Mary's death, and Luke had dreaded going. Then Anita had taken the stage and everything in the room had seemed to transform. "You weren't Cher, but you weren't bad, you know."

"That was only because I fortified myself with several marga—" She cut off the words, realizing there was an impressionable teen in the room. "Well, that's a story for another day. My point was that there are an awful lot of things you can learn from the accounts of history. These people all had lives like you do, lives that were turned upside down and inside out by the choices they made or circumstances they didn't ask for." Anita leaned past Emily, typed in a few words, clicked the mouse and whizzed through cyberspace. "It might be easier to look at your history lessons as enormous works of fiction. If you see people like Winston Churchill as characters, it becomes fun to find out the ending to his story."

Emily leaned back in her chair. "I never thought of it that way."

"Here, try this site. There's a lot of great information about World War II there. I wrote an article on a group of veterans before I left L.A. and did some of my research here." She slid the computer over to Emily, relating a few other Web addresses for research and then put the girl in control.

"Cool!" Emily leaned forward, using the computer with one hand and scribbling notes with the other.

Anita pivoted again in her chair and her skirt hiked up another couple of inches.

Luke jerked his gaze away and concentrated on the least-sexy thing in the room. A squat cookie jar shaped like a pug, complete with a ceramic chefs' hat and smirky dog grin. *Think cookies,* he told himself. *Chocolate chip, peanut butter, macadamia nut…*

Before he could get to thumbprints cookies, his gaze was back on Anita's fabulous legs. His concentration was shot, at least as long as Anita was here. And that was dangerous. Very dangerous.

She was pregnant, he reminded himself. By another man. Luke had his own problems to worry about. Thinking about Anita in any way other than as a friend he used to know was bad. And even though his curiosity about why she was here and why she was having a baby by herself was damn near eating him up, he didn't ask, at least not while his daughter was in the room.

Anita rose and crossed to him. "She's doing great with the computer." Anita leaned close, her voice a whisper. "But maybe we should leave her alone so she doesn't feel like we're watching over her shoulder.'' Anita smiled. ''And then she'd stop working, just to spite you.''

He smiled back. ''You know her too well.''

She shrugged. ''Hey, I was twelve once, too.''

Luke motioned to Anita to follow him across the hall and into the den. When she sat in one of the armchairs, her skirt hiked up again.

Luke took the chair opposite and tried like hell to keep his gaze on her face.

''We really shouldn't tie up your laptop or your time,'' he said, in a lame attempt at a coherent conversation. ''Emily can use my computer.''

''It's no big deal,'' Anita said. ''Besides, it's still pouring out. I'll go to the library when it stops raining.''

In that case, Luke hoped Mercy was in for a flood.

''And I know you, Luke. You don't like anyone messing with your computer.'' Anita grinned. ''You treat that thing like some people treat their Pomeranians.''

The laughter that rose in his throat and then escaped him had such a foreign sound that for a brief second, Luke almost didn't recognize it. ''I guess I do. Never get between a man and his computer,'' he quipped.

''I'll remember that.'' Her voice had taken on a deeper tone, as if she was remembering the same moment he was. A late night in his office, both of them tired from working on a project all day, sharing a few cartons of delivered Chinese, laughing, joking, then not joking at all, Anita's body pressed against his desk, her mouth hungrily tasting his, equipment falling to the floor as Luke tried to get closer, touch more of her, the blinding passion driving him like the engine of a two-ton truck.

Luke cleared his throat and got to his feet, putting some distance between himself and the jasmine perfume triggering memories in his mind like a starting pistol. He fiddled with the line of framed photos on the mantel.

"So, what do you think of Mercy so far?"

She laughed. "It's not exactly L.A."

"Hey, we have a strip mall. And two stoplights. We're civilized."

She laughed. "Compared to California, this is the outback."

He leaned against the doorframe, trying to look nonchalant in a white short-sleeved shirt and khaki shorts. He suspected he resembled an ironing board more than anything else. "I take it our tiny town bores a city girl like you."

Anita turned toward the sound of Luke's voice and concentrated only on the deep, rich timbre. Luke Dole had a measured way of speaking that was both direct and calming, like the roll of the ocean as the tide came in. "No, not at all," she said quietly. "It's exactly what I was looking for."

He hadn't moved from his spot against the doorjamb, the seemingly relaxed pose masking obvious tension. The muscles in his neck were stiff and his easy grin was anything but.

He seemed unnerved by her presence, as if he was afraid she'd bring up that night—that crazy, heated night in his office—in front of his daughter. Anita might not be the classiest woman in the world, but she was far from tactless. And she wasn't the kind to whine and demand explanations. A year ago, he'd made it clear, and she'd agreed, that nothing would come of their kiss. Leaving it that way was best for both of them.

Besides, she didn't need a relationship right now. Anita didn't rely on other people. Men especially. All a man would do was complicate her plans, a lesson she'd learned in her relationship with Nicholas. Anita pressed a palm to her stomach, knowing her new life, her entire world really, was right inside.

Anita clasped her hands together, feeling oddly uncomfortable. It took a minute for her to realize why—she'd always had a business-based relationship with Luke. Never had she been in his home, or in any kind of private area with him, except for that one hot, wild evening in his office. She cleared her throat, looking for common ground. "So, how's Mark?"

Luke grinned. "Married, believe it or not."

"Mark?" She couldn't hide the surprise in her voice. "I thought he was set on being the world's oldest bachelor."

"So did he. Then he met Claire, and he was hooked."

"Claire? As in Claire Richards? The one who used to live in my house?"

"Yep. The very same one. They fell in love in an RV." Anita's eyes widened and Luke let out a laugh. "It's a long story. Remind me to tell you sometime."

"I will," she said, softer than she'd intended. Between them, the temperature rose and the silence thickened.

"So…" he said after a pause, "what brought you to Mercy? Work?"

She laughed. "Actually, I'm not working much at all right now. I quit my job in L.A. when I got pregnant, and now I'm becoming…well, sort of an entrepreneur. With booties."

"Booties?" He looked about as stunned as he had when she hit him with the Teflon.

"Long story," she parroted.

"Maybe you'll tell me over dinner sometime?"

She saw the surprise that flitted across his features, as if he'd shocked himself by asking her out. "I don't think that would be a good idea. I mean, well…" she let the words trail off because she didn't know quite what she did mean. Images of sitting across a table from Luke in a darkened restaurant, sharing a plate of linguini, tasting and teasing, played at the edges of her mind.

"Yeah, you're probably right," he finished for her.

Anita got to her feet, stretching her back and arms. As soon as she moved, her stomach began to rumble in an ironic twist that belied her refusal for dinner. The last thing she'd had to eat was that god-awful marmalade. Must have been Luke's mention of dinner that set her off. That, and the hungry life inside her.

Ever since she'd gotten pregnant, it seemed as if her life revolved around the thought of food. Pickles, French fries, Twinkies. Sometimes, in the middle of the night, she'd start craving some crazy treat and end up driving around, searching for a convenience store that had stockpiles of Hostess goodies.

"I should probably go," she said to Luke, heading toward the hall. "I'll leave my laptop here so Emily doesn't lose all the bookmarks and page histories. I can pick it up later." Her stomach rumbled again, like a complaining volcano.

"Hungry?"

She felt her face heat up. She paused in the doorway to the kitchen. Luke was inches behind her. "Yeah, a little. Okay, a lot. It's all right, though. I have some ham at home."

"Let me guess. From the Mercy Welcoming Committee?" He laughed and the sound of it was like a fresh cup of espresso, vibrant and full. "Stay away from Miss Tanner's homemade marmalade. She has to give the stuff away to strangers because it's so awful. She's a legend at the Indiana State Fair."

Anita grimaced. "That's one lesson I already learned. Even the mouse wouldn't touch that stuff."

"Listen, the rain isn't about to let up any time soon. Why don't you stay for dinner? With me and my family. No strings, no dates."

"I shouldn't—"

Luke gestured toward his daughter, still excitedly surfing the Net and jotting notes. "It looks like Emily has hit upon a gold mine of information and isn't ready to let go of your laptop yet. Afterward, I can take a look at your car."

"I can't just impose like that—"

Luke lowered his mouth to her ear. "I haven't seen my daughter do a lick of homework for the last six months. Whatever magic touch you seem to have, I'm hoping you'll stay until she's finished that report.''

His breath was warm on her ears, rocketing her back to that night he'd kissed her, the one time Anita had followed her instincts, not her head. Desire to taste that slice of heaven again pulsed through her.

Staying here, with Luke, was a crazy idea. He was the kind of man she'd vowed to avoid—a workaholic who would invariably get swept up into the office and forget she existed. She'd learned a long time ago that she could do virtually anything on her own. She depended on herself, no one else. Getting involved with Luke would just be retreading familiar ground.

She thought about saying no, came up with at least ten different ways of refusing, then caught a glimpse of steaks defrosting on the counter, flanked by a row of potatoes.

Steak. Potatoes. With butter. Sour cream.

Her mouth began to water at the sight of the food, even uncooked. She wasn't much of a cook—heck, she'd barely mastered her microwave—and it had been a long time since she'd eaten anything that hadn't come out of a box or a can. Even longer since she'd shared a meal with a family.

Longing sprang to life within Anita, reaching out fingers that grasped her heart and tugged at her to stay. When she'd been little, she'd passed the long hours of her childhood in front of the television, watching reruns of *Happy Days*.

But, back then, what she'd craved more than food was the warm comfort of the Cunningham living room and the way they'd always welcomed Fonzie, a near stranger, into their hearts and kitchen. Even now, watching the show brought all those feelings rushing back.

Anita shook her head, dismissing the memory. For Pete's sake, she was nearly thirty now, well past the age where she needed a mother to lay out cookies and a glass of milk at the end of the day.

Before she could answer Luke, the back door opened and in a flurry of packages and barking dogs, a woman entered.

"Gracious! What a day!" She deposited the packages on the counter and offered a quick stroke to each of the three dogs who circled her in a joyful frenzy. "Hello, Emily. How nice to see you doing your homework!" The petite gray-haired woman, clad in jeans and a huge red-and-white sweatshirt that read I'm 4 I. U., patted Emily's shoulder affectionately. "Luke, dear, would you give me a hand with the groceries? There are a few bags in the trunk." She handed him her keys and then paused in her bustle of chatter and movement to contemplate Anita. "Why, hello. I don't think we've met. I'm Grace Dole."

"Anita Ricardo," Anita responded, shaking the proffered hand. This gregarious, bundle-of-energy woman was quiet, contemplative Luke's mother? It seemed so improbable that Anita thought of asking to see the birth certificate.

"Oh, I remember your name." She nodded, sweeping an appraising gaze over Anita's form. "Luke and Mark used to rave about you when you were working with them."

"They did?" Anita blinked. She didn't allow herself to wonder whether Luke had raved about her for any reason besides her marketing skills.

"Anita is so rad, Grandma," Emily said, scrambling to her feet and pointing first to Anita and then to the computer. "She hooked me up and slapped a load of four-one-one on me for my report."

Sixtyish Grace laughed and raised her palm, giving her granddaughter a high five. "That is way cool, Em."

The joyful sound of laughter rang through the room. Even the three spaniels joined in, adding a chorus of approving barks.

"Mom, when did you learn to speak Preteen?" Luke asked, shaking his head and still chuckling softly as he carried in several grocery bags. "Half of what Emily says sounds more like Greek than English to me."

Grace tilted her chin and put on an air of mock superiority. "I am one hip grandma. I even wear Skechers." She held up a foot to show off her youthful sneakers.

"Next you'll be raiding my closet, Grandma," Emily said, laughing more. "Geez, I haven't laughed like that since—" She cut off midsentence.

Luke drew in a breath. A shadow washed across his face.

Like a heavy wool blanket, somber silence fell over the room. Emily's gaze dropped to the floor, Luke's to some faraway spot outside the window. Sympathy shimmered in Grace's eyes.

Anita was uncomfortably aware that she was an outsider, peeking in on what was surely a very private moment of grieving. These were shared memories she shouldn't have access to. The best thing to do was slip away and leave the Doles alone. But there was no tactful way to grab her computer and dash out the door.

"Well," Grace said finally, "let's get these steaks and potatoes on the grill. I brought home some tomatoes and cucumbers to make a salad. Anita, could you chop these and toss them into a bowl with the lettuce?" Grace held out a bag of plump, ripe tomatoes and pointed Anita toward a cutting board and knife that lay on the opposite counter.

"I should go—"

"Nonsense." Grace placed the tomatoes in Anita's palms and closed her hands gently over them. "It's suppertime and you're already here. Stay." Grace wagged a finger at her. "All I ask is that you pitch in with the dishes, not try to sneak out the back door like my boys always do." She raised an eyebrow toward Luke.

"My mother likes to exaggerate." Luke sent a grin in Anita's direction that slid through her like honey in tea, before he turned back toward Grace. "If I remember right, I had dishpan hands a lot more often than Mark did."

Grace reached up and patted Luke's cheek. "That's because you were the one I could always depend on. Loyal Luke, I called you." And then she smiled, the kind of smile that seemed part of some special mother-child language.

Anita turned away and busied herself removing the tomatoes from the bag and scrubbing them under the faucet. A lump rose in her throat and her chest felt tight, as if she might hyperventilate on the spot.

She didn't belong here. She should leave. Head for the library. Immerse herself in work until she was too tired to do anything but sleep.

But her legs refused to move. And her hands kept washing the tomatoes, then patting them dry with a paper towel.

Grace steered Luke to Anita's side, depositing a pair of cucumbers, a second knife and a cutting board before him. "Slice these and help fix the salad." She wagged a finger at him. "And don't forget to toss it. A good salad is a mixture, not a bunch of layers."

"You can't blame me for liking things nice and neat."

"You redefine neatness, Luke," his mother laughed. "I've always told you life is messy, so don't keep trying to arrange it like a stack of dominoes. And don't you dare make my salad look like a work of art."

He grinned and leaned toward Anita's ear. "My mother's all bark and no bite."

"I heard that, Lucas. Behave yourself," Grace said. She smiled at him, then laid a soft, momentary touch on Anita's shoulder. "And make our guest feel at home."

And just like that, Anita Ricardo was welcomed into the Dole kitchen.

Just like Fonzie.

Chapter Four

There should be a law against perfumes that smelled that good. Anything distracting enough to make a razor-sharp knife slip out of Luke's hands, not once, but twice, should definitely be banned.

Truth be told, it wasn't just the scent of jasmine that rattled Luke. It was the woman who wore the scent. Anita.

She stood silent beside him, slicing the tomatoes and piling them on the cutting board. If anything, the quiet, punctuated by Emily's fingers typing on the laptop and the excited yips of the dogs chasing each other's tails around the kitchen, just heightened all his other senses.

Like smell. Touch. Sight. Out of the corner of his eye, he could see her. The near-butterscotch color of her skin, the long dark hair that curled around her shoulders and brushed her bare skin like delicate fingers. The sundress, skimming along her form with familiarity.

Anita was at least a foot away but the radar of his skin was attuned to her every movement.

He finished the cucumbers. Finally. Granted, the vegetables looked as if they'd been sliced by a five-year-old with a chop saw, but at least they were done. There was no longer any reason to stand so close to Anita. He should have been happy and left her to finish assembling the dish.

Instead, he took a step closer, scooped the slices up and loaded them into the bowl. "Let's get this salad made." He reached for her pile of tomatoes.

Anita's hands jetted out at the same time, brushing against his. The moment of contact sent a surge of electricity through him. He glanced at her. Their gazes met and held for just an instant, but it was enough to tell him that she'd been zapped just as hard.

"I, ah, like your pug," she said.

"Pug?" Was that some term for a piece of his anatomy that he'd missed in High School Sex 101?

"You know, the cookie jar?" She gestured toward the squat ceramic dog on the counter.

"Oh! Yeah, that. My mother made it in her ceramics phase."

"Ceramics phase?"

"My mom's what she likes to call a scattered crafter. One month it's macramé, another it's stained glass." He patted the glossy dog's head. "Charlie here is from her pre-knitting days."

"Cute."

Did she mean him? Or the dog? *Duh,* as Emily

would say. The answer was obvious. How could he compete with a painted pet filled with chocolate chip cookies? "If you're still here at Christmas, you'll likely end up with a Grace Dole Creation of your own."

Where the hell did that come from? It was August. Why was he talking about Anita and Christmas?

"Handmade is nice," she said.

"Oh come on. You're an L.A. girl. The only thing handmade out there is the signal to the valet to get your car."

She laughed. "I'm not living that life anymore. I've changed."

He allowed himself one slow, piercing look at her. His heart rate accelerated, his hands itched to reach out and scoop her up, vegetables be damned. "You have. Very much. No more high heels, no more power suits."

"No more job," she said. She let out a short hiccup of a laugh. "Different things are important to me now."

"I can see that," Luke said, his voice so quiet it almost hummed.

"How's that salad coming?" Grace asked.

Anita jerked back, away from Luke. "All done." She grabbed up the stack of tomatoes and dumped them into the bowl then hurried over to the sink to wash her hands.

"Almost. We forgot to mix," Luke said. He began tossing the salad with two large spoons.

Oh, they hadn't forgotten to mix, Anita thought. They were mixing like peas and carrots in a blender.

What was she doing? Sitting down with Luke at the dinner table as if she belonged here? As if they were a family?

She was a realist. That meant she didn't fool herself with fairy-tale dreams about nuclear families and knights on white horses. That didn't happen, at least not for her.

Anita wiped her hands over and over on the dish towel. A twinge of desire still lingered within her from his touch and his quiet husky words about how she'd changed. He'd meant more than her shoes, that was for sure.

Letting her body rule her brain was emotional suicide. The last thing she came to Mercy to do was to meet a man, or reunite with *this* man. She was here to raise her baby, to form her own little family of two. Nothing more. Not now.

She laid the towel on the counter. "You know, I've barely finished unpacking. I should go and leave you all to your meal."

"What, and miss having some of our creation?" Luke held out the bowl of salad. His tone held a hint of a tease in it, as if daring her to stay. "Besides, if you leave now, my mother will never forgive you."

"I—I—"

"Not to mention, there's a rib eye out there with your name on it." Luke pointed at the grill Grace was tending under the patio awning. Puffs of smoke waffled from the top. "If you think my mother is good with pugs, you should see her with beef."

Anita laughed. "I just feel weird. Intruding and all."

"You're not intruding." Luke came closer and placed the glass salad bowl into her hands. "We're just two old friends, getting together for a meal. Right?"

"Uh-huh."

"Good." His cobalt-blue gaze held her, a steady, heated magnet. "I'm glad we got that settled."

Anita swallowed. "Yeah, me, too."

If that was the case, then why did she have an overpowering urge to reach out, grab Luke and haul him to her so she could taste a heck of a lot more than steak?

Hormones. That's what it was. Nothing a ten-pound Hershey's bar couldn't cure.

Anita glanced at the bowl in her hands. Not a drop of chocolate in there.

Eating a tossed salad to calm hormonal cravings was about as effective as using a water pistol to halt a charging rhino. Anita had a sneaking suspicion the pug was going to lose a little of his girth before the evening was over.

While the potatoes and steak sizzled on the barbecue, Luke took the coward's way out and retreated to his computer. Anita was a few feet away, working with Emily. After their salad conversation—if that's what he could call it—he'd been left feeling off-kilter, as if some puberty switch had been flicked on in his brain.

Hormones, nothing more. Just a bit too much testosterone. Nothing a little red meat couldn't cure.

Luke sat at his desk in the alcove with every intention of working, but not a single line of code made it from his brain and onto the screen. All he saw when he looked at that blinking cursor was Anita, pulsing in and out of his line of vision on his right.

She wasn't having any trouble concentrating. He could see her to his right, across the room, laughing and talking with Emily. Luke squared his shoulders, laid his fingers on the keys and typed.

Gibberish. A half page of nothing but jumbled letters, as if he'd put his fingers in the wrong place, QWERTY be damned.

"That's great, Emily! That will add some real depth to your report. Now what about…" Anita's voice became muffled when she stood and leaned over to make some marks on the notepad beside Emily.

Had she no idea what happened to that perky little floral skirt when she bent over like that?

Luke let out a gust and went back to the screen. Blink, blink. The computer seemed to be staring at him, as if saying, *well, when are you going to do something?*

He ran a hand through his hair and settled into the hard maple chair. Then he reached forward, adjusted his monitor by three millimeters, turned the keyboard a half degree to the left and replaced his fingers on the keys.

Blink, blink.

"Dinner's ready," his mother called.

"Thank God," Luke muttered. He pushed back his chair and got to his feet. Anita straightened, too, and the yellow sundress slid down her legs and back into place. He should have been happy it wasn't riding up her hips anymore.

But what he should be thinking and what he actually thought were two very different things.

She glanced over her shoulder at him, clear brown eyes locking on his for the briefest of seconds. Just before she turned away, a slight smile curved across her face in a slow, almost sultry crescent.

She might as well have smacked him with a CPU. He blinked several times. When was the last time a woman had made him feel like that? Like he'd been punched in the gut?

He'd spent two years being numb, feeling nothing, except for that one night in his office. He'd perfected the art of staying above emotion. He'd learned long ago that making decisions based on his emotions led to very stupid choices. Ones where other people got hurt, not just him.

And now, in the space of a few hours, Anita had walked into his life and shocked his heart back into life. A good thing? Or not?

Definitely not. Emily was his priority. And yet, a tiny part of him—controlled by that overelectrified puberty switch—cried out for some attention, too.

Later. Now, work and Emily, nothing else.

He turned into the dining room and took a seat in the antique oak chair across from Anita. Her head was down and she was fumbling a bit with the napkin on her lap, trying to get it centered across her belly. Emily opted to sit beside Anita, casting Luke a glare. The family dinner was not high on Emily's list of favorite things to do.

Grace bustled in with a platter of food, placed it in the center of the table and then sat down. "I hope you all are starving," she said. "We have lots of steak."

"You always make too much food, Mom," Luke said. "That's one of the good things about staying here."

"Don't want anyone saying I don't feed my kids," she said. She glanced at Anita. "Or my guests."

"It's been a long time since I had a meal like this." Anita swept a hand across the table. "You might have to hold me back from grabbing for thirds."

Grace laughed. "I brought up four boys. A big appetite is a requirement around this place."

"Good thing, since I'm eating for two," Anita said.

The back door opened and Luke's father walked into the house, pausing to wash his hands before he entered the dining room. John stopped first at the other end of the table, pressing a kiss to Grace's cheek. "What's for dinner, Gracie?"

His wife smiled back at him, a tease on her lips. "For you, maybe sloppy joes. For the rest of us, rib eyes and potatoes."

"Aw, shoot. My turn to cook tonight, wasn't it? I forgot. Got tied up at Henry's, working on his kitchen cabinets. Banged up my hand pretty damned good, too, on those stupid doors he—" John stopped when his gaze lighted on Anita. "Apparently I left my manners over there, too. Sorry." He thrust out a hand to her. "John Dole."

"Anita Ricardo," Anita said, shaking his hand. She cast a quick glance across the table. "Luke's...friend."

Friend? What word had he been hoping to hear? Girlfriend? Past marketing consultant? None of those defined their relationship now.

In fact, they didn't even have a relationship. She lived in the same town as he did. That was all.

The platter came around to him. Luke slid a steak and a foil-wrapped potato onto his plate before passing the dish to his mother. He dived into the food. Anything to get his mind off the woman sitting across from him.

"So, Anita, what brought you to Mercy?" Grace asked.

Anita swallowed the bite of steak in her mouth. "Actually, Luke."

Grace and John both glanced at their son, then at Anita's abdomen. He felt like holding up a sign that said Not Me but anyone who did the math—he'd been in Mercy over a year now and Anita only looked about six or seven months pregnant—could see he'd had nothing to do with that baby.

"He told me so much about this place when we worked together that it made me want to move here. It seems like the perfect place to raise my child."

Luke could see the questions in his mother's eyes. Grace, however, was nothing if not polite and she didn't ask about the father of the baby. "You'll love Mercy and I'm sure Mercy will love you, too."

"That's what I'm hoping," Anita said quietly.

"You left L.A. for here?" John asked. "You're

going to miss the beach, come winter. I'm always telling Gracie we need to retire to Florida.''

"We're taking that cruise later this week for our anniversary, John." Grace dropped a dollop of sour cream onto her potato. "I bet by the end of the trip, you'll be complaining up and down about the heat."

"The heat you and I are going to create together?" John quirked an eyebrow at her.

Grace flushed a bit. "Little pitchers have big ears, remember?''

"Grandma, I'm twelve." Emily's voice was filled with preteen exasperation. "I know what sex is."

When had his daughter gotten so old? And where did she learn about sex? Definitely not a topic he wanted to pursue, especially not when his own thoughts had been running down that road every time he looked at Anita. "Eat your dinner," Luke ordered.

Emily responded by pushing the food around her plate with her fork. "You know I don't eat anything with a face, Dad. I'm a vegan." She scrunched up her nose and laid the fork down. "Besides, I think it's disgusting to carve up cows and slap them on a plate for dinner."

"Emily!" Luke glanced at his parents, then directed a hard look at his daughter. "Grandma and Grandpa worked hard to provide this food for you. Don't disrespect them."

"Well, it's true, isn't it? Somebody had to herd those poor innocent cows into a chute and then let the machine—"

"*That* is quite enough," Luke said, cutting her off

before she reached the more graphic parts of meat processing.

"Emily," Anita cut in, "why don't you tell your father how your report is coming?"

"Fine." Emily kept her gaze glued to the table-cloth.

"It's more than fine. You've got some really interesting research there, and I was pretty impressed with your writing skills. I know journalists who can't put a sentence together as creatively as you did in that introduction."

Emily raised her head and turned to Anita. The small amount of praise shone in her eyes. "You…you really think I did a good job?"

Anita smiled and nodded. "This one's an A in the making, for sure."

"I've always liked to write." The admission slipped softly from Emily's lips. "I love J. K. Rowling's books. It'd be cool to do that."

"The second Harry Potter was my favorite," Anita said. "Have you read all of the series?"

"Oh yeah. I especially liked the third one when Harry and Hermione…" Emily launched into a long description of her favorite scene. Anita nodded and interjected details she remembered from the tale, as well.

Luke's gaze shifted from his daughter to Anita. Had an alien landed on the dining room table? Or was that really his daughter, admitting to liking writing and having a conversation about an author?

Anita wasn't just an angel, she was a godsend. After dinner, he intended to make her an offer she couldn't refuse. And on the off chance she did say no, he'd sweeten the pot somehow. Whatever it took, Luke didn't care.

Anita was the answer he'd been looking for.

Anita had known Luke long enough to know when he had something on his mind. After dinner, she'd helped clear the table and wash the dishes, chattering with Grace about the town and the best place to shop for groceries. Luke's mother had a warm and giving personality. She talked with Anita as if she were a longtime member of the family.

Almost like a daughter.

Warmth spread through Anita, not because she had a good meal in her, not because her hands were in and out of the soapy dishwater, but because of Grace.

A little voice inside reminded her that the Doles were not her family. It was one dinner, one evening. It didn't mean anything.

Don't get too close. Don't get too comfortable.

Luke hovered in the back of the kitchen, flipping through papers and jotting notes. When the dishes were done, he came over and took the towel from Anita's hands. "I'll bring you home and work on your car for you. My dad hurt his hand, so you're stuck with me."

"Do you know anything about engines?"

"Enough. You don't grow up in this house without pitching in on everything from the station wagon to the laundry. I wouldn't attempt to change out a transmission, but I can do some basic stuff."

"Okay. I can't afford a mechanic right now, so that

sounds like a good deal to me. Let me just grab my things.''

A few minutes later, Anita and Luke were alone in his Chevy, heading for her rental house. He didn't say much on the short drive, just pointed out a few landmarks and noted the hours of the library when she asked about it. He kept both hands on the wheel, exactly at ten and two, as if he didn't want to risk touching her—or losing control.

He swung into the driveway and put the car in park. The rain had stopped and when Anita got out, the first thing she noticed was how clean the air smelled, as if the town had been washed. A leafy elm tree hung heavily over the drive, its branches reaching out and brushing against the house, almost as if it was welcoming them home. The lawns were thick and green again, flowers blooming in the yard next door. The sky was a cornflower blue, clear as a crayon. ''It's beautiful here,'' she said.

''A bit too quiet for me, but yes, it is beautiful.'' Luke reached in, took out her laptop and umbrella, then followed her up the walkway to the house.

''This is going to sound corny to you, but it's almost like seeing God's hand at work when you look out over the landscape. In L.A., everything's all concrete and steel. Mother Nature is hard to find among the skyscrapers and freeways. But here…'' Anita took in another breath, wrapping her arms around her chest and pivoting on the grass. ''It's like you can see how the world came to be.''

''Give it a month. When you can't find a store open on Sunday or when the telephone service goes out for the third time in a week, you'll have quite a different opinion of Mercy.''

Anita shook her head. ''I don't think so. I'm—'' she smiled, placed a hand on her abdomen ''—we're here to stay.''

Luke lowered her things to the porch swing. He gazed at her for a long silent second. ''It's nice to see you again, Anita.'' He swallowed, his eyes never leaving hers. ''Very nice.''

''I've thought about you a lot over the last eighteen months.'' There. She'd said it. ''Wondering how you were.''

''Hanging in. It's about all I can do.''

''Yeah.'' She reached forward to touch him, to lay a hand of comfort on his arm, but then her hand connected with his bare skin and the comfort she meant to offer became something altogether different. She held his gaze, a question in her eyes that she didn't know how to ask.

''I should…I should take a look at your car before it gets too dark.''

''Oh yeah. Right.'' Anita stepped back, releasing him. ''It's right over there.'' She dug the keys out of her purse and dropped them into his hand. His fingers closed over the metal and he paused, as if he meant to say something. Then the moment passed and Luke trundled down the porch steps and over to the Toyota.

Anita rubbed the back of her neck. What had she been thinking? Why had she touched him like that? Hadn't she learned already that playing with fire just left her heart charred to a crisp?

She sat on the swing, pushing off with her feet.

The breeze from the movement cooled her a bit. Anita closed her eyes and leaned her head against the wooden slats.

She should have never come here. Never moved within three blocks of him. There were hundreds of other towns she could have chosen. But none of them held Luke. And as much as she tried to tell herself she didn't care or didn't want a relationship with him...

She did.

She saw how he looked at his daughter. The love in his eyes. The clear fatherly concern he had. Sure, they had trouble getting along now, but that was to be expected after what the two of them had been through and what was coming as Emily entered her teenage years. Beneath all the eye rolling and arguing, though, Anita could see the love.

Luke was a good man. She'd known it the minute she met him. Back then, he'd belonged to another. And he'd been grieving.

But now, he wasn't. And he didn't belong to any woman at all.

Those kinds of thoughts just led to T-R-O-U-B-L-E.

Anita stopped the swing, got to her feet and went into the house. She flicked a switch, sent up an alleluia that the electricity was working, then mixed up a glass of instant lemonade for Luke, adding the last of the ice from the cooler.

She told herself, while she stirred, that all she was doing was bringing him a friendly glass of refreshment. Because it was hot outside. And he was doing her a favor. She wasn't thinking about getting involved with him. She wasn't flirting with him.

He might be a good man, but even good men left. Even good men let you down. She'd already had enough disappointment for one life. She wasn't about to ask for more.

He had taken off his shirt and was shoulder deep under the hood of the Toyota. Anita held her breath, to keep from panting aloud. She'd never seen this angle of Luke before and had to admit, it was a nice one.

Mighty nice.

Okay, *that* was definitely not a disappointment.

Nothing like a guy with his shirt off to get her hormones raring like a driver at the start of the Indy 500. Her pulse revved when she took a step closer to Luke. Her resolve about keeping her distance from him melted in the summer heat and at the shock of seeing Luke bare chested.

Deliver the lemonade and don't slobber all over him.

The muscles in his back flexed and released as he adjusted this and that, pulling tools from a tool chest he must have brought in his car.

"I...I, ah, thought you might want this," she said.

He jerked upward, bumping his head on the hood. He turned, rubbing the sore spot. "I think I should start wearing a helmet when you're around."

"Sorry, didn't mean to scare you." Lord, his chest was even better than his back. Lean ripples of muscle tapering down to a narrow waist, a deep rich tan making every inch of his skin glow against the paleness of his khaki shorts. She thrust out the glass before she dropped it. "Here."

"You are a goddess." He swiped his forehead with the back of his hand then took the glass and downed it in one big gulp. "I thought the rain was going to break this heat wave, but it only seemed to make it worse."

She hoped like heck it would be too hot for him to wear a shirt for the next, oh, thirty or forty days. "You still running and working out?"

He nodded. "Six miles a day."

"I can tell." Had she just said that? Might as well start drooling at his feet. "I meant—"

"Hey, I think you just complimented me. Don't ruin it by qualifying what you said." He laid the glass on the ground. "It's been a while since I've been flattered by a woman."

"I don't know why. I mean, you're a good-looking guy, Luke."

He shrugged. "I don't get out much."

"Oh." She toyed with the appliqué flower on her neckline. "Aren't you dating anyone?"

"I haven't dated since—" He looked away. "No."

"Oh." The air between them grew tight, thick. Anita looked for something to do. "You have a bit of grease—" she grabbed a rag from the toolbox "—right there." She raised herself up on her tiptoes and swiped the cloth across his cheek. The grease only smeared. She took a step forward and rubbed at it again.

Luke's chest rose and fell between them. His breath hitched. Anita had to force herself to concentrate on her task. His cologne, a blend of citrus and sage, teased at her, a temptation to come closer. "I can't seem to get it—"

And then, his mouth was on hers, his arms around her, in one massive swoop. Just like the first time. An eruption of want, more powerful than either one of them.

Chapter Five

His lips moved against hers, as if he were mapping territory in an insatiable hunger to possess more. She reached up, pulling at him, the rag dropping to the ground, her heart throbbing in her chest. She curved against his six-foot height with ease, as if she were made for him.

His fingers splayed across her back, meeting bare skin above the edge of her dress and setting off another fire inside her. How long had it been since she'd been touched? Kissed? Loved?

Forever.

He tasted of after-dinner coffee and long pent-up desire. She couldn't remember anymore why she'd decided not to get close to him. He felt so right, so perfect.

She'd known him for so long that touching Luke was both a surprise and a comfort, as if she was coming home after years away from a place she'd missed.

She tangled her hands in his hair, pulling his head down, asking for more of him. More of everything.

He spun her around, pressing her to the car, his hardness against her a clear telegraph of how swiftly the desire had hit him, too. She leaned into him, need pulsing through her, hearing nothing but the roar of desire. Their mouths and hands connected and consumed in a wild, beatless tango. Anita closed her eyes, gave herself up to the feelings.

To Luke.

He jerked back suddenly and whirled away from her. Anita opened her eyes, blinked in the sudden harsh light of the setting sun. She touched a finger to her swollen lips. The feeling of his mouth still lingered, like the scent of pine after the Christmas tree was taken down. Sweet and nostalgic and nearly making her weak in the knees.

"That shouldn't have happened," he said. His voice sounded as if it was buried under a ton of gravel. "I'm sorry."

"I didn't say no, Luke. I wanted that kiss as much as you did." She stepped forward and placed a hand on his back. "It's okay to kiss me."

He heaved a sigh. "You don't want to get involved with me. I'm not going down that road again. With anyone."

"I know it's been hard since your wife died, but—"

"But I can't." He bent over, picked up the rag and wiped his palms, then draped it over the side of the car. He placed his hands on either side of the engine and lowered his head. "What happened just now was—'' He shook his head. ''Crazy. I let it get out of hand. For the second time, too. I'm sorry. I've just been alone a long time and…''

''Luke, I understand.''

''No, you don't. I have a lot on my shoulders right now. I can't get involved with you, or anyone else.'' He let out a breath. ''I don't know if a relationship would be a good idea.''

''Whoa!'' She put up her hands. ''I kissed you, you kissed me. I'm not talking about marching down the aisle or anything right now. Do you want to know why you kissed me?''

He straightened. ''I know why I kissed you.''

''Because you want me,'' she answered for him. ''And I kissed you for the same reason. Face it. Neither one of us has forgotten that kiss in your office.''

He swallowed, his gaze on her lips. ''No, I don't think we have.''

''So, we had a little…unfinished business.''

''Is that what that was?''

''Yes. And now, you're running scared.''

''I'm not scared.''

''Oh, yes, you are.'' She stepped forward, pointing a finger at his chest. ''You are terrified of me. And all the rest of what you said, it's just an excuse to go crawl into your shell. I know you, Luke, better than you think.''

''I don't crawl into a shell.''

''You do, too. You retreat into work and you pretend the world doesn't exist. I'm attracted to you. I'm not going to lie and pretend I'm not, but I'm not foolish enough to have a relationship with you. I know you and I know what you're like." She tapped on his torso. "You, my friend, are a turtle."

"Gee, I think I liked it better when you were complimenting my body."

She smiled. "Okay, a turtle with a nice shell then." She ran a hand down the side of the car, her gaze averted from his. "So, as long as we're clear on this now. No romantic relationship. Just friends."

"Yeah, just friends."

"Good." She nodded, convincing herself that this was exactly what she'd wanted. Wasn't it? "Perfect." Then she spun on her heel and left.

Well, that went well.

He might as well just smack himself across the head with the toolbox and be done with it. Luke considered going after her, but figured it would be best if he kept his distance.

He hated to admit she was right. Anita had nailed him with pinpoint accuracy. He might as well face facts.

He was a turtle.

He bent down inside the car again. He concentrated on wires and plugs, distributor caps and air valves. An hour later, he climbed inside the Toyota, turned the key and was rewarded by the sound of the engine cranking over.

He'd probably ruined his friendship with Anita— and any hope of her helping him with Emily—by kissing her. It was kind of like trying to stuff the genie back into the bottle. Couldn't be done. They'd taken their relationship to another level, and even though she'd said they'd be friends again, he knew that was impossible. He doubted he'd ever be able to look at her and think of "friend" again. That word was reserved for the guys he shared a beer and pizza with. Not someone who kissed like Jeff Gordon drove—with wild abandon, careening around the course with no regard for speed or rules.

He might not be able to repair the damage to his friendship with Anita, but he could get her car running again. For a man who seemed to do his best to screw up relationships, it was something.

Anita didn't come outside again, not even when her car started. He shut off the engine, loaded up his tools, put his shirt back on, then crossed to her front door. He had to find a way to repair this mess, too, if his plan to help Em was going to work. He rang the bell and waited. No answer. He rang it again.

"Thank you for fixing my car."

Luke swiveled and saw Anita leaning out the window. She dipped her head, then slipped one leg out, her dress riding clear up to her hips.

Oh, Lord.

He forgot to avert his eyes. Well, maybe not *forgot*. Before he could see much more than a long, creamy leg, she had the other leg through and was standing on the porch, skirt back in place. Damn.

She pointed at the door. "The knob is broken. Plus, the door gets stuck in the humidity. The window works just as well." She laughed. "At least until this heat wave breaks."

He scowled. "You shouldn't be climbing in and

out of a window all day. You're what, six months pregnant?''

"Seven.'' She shrugged. "I'm okay. I'm pretty agile. All those jazzercise classes I used to take.''

"Listen—'' he flipped the keys in his hand a few times before continuing ''—I was a jerk back there. Let's call a truce. I'll fix your door and then maybe we can talk about you repaying me with a different favor.''

She arched an eyebrow.

"No, no. I didn't mean anything like that.'' Yet his mind traveled down that path anyway, picturing Anita in his arms again, her mouth on his, her long, delicate fingers bringing all those dead parts of him back to life. He threw up a mental Stop sign before he caused a collision between his libido and his best intentions. "Something to do with Emily.''

Anita's clear brown gaze considered him for a minute. She looked…almost disappointed when he'd clarified the favor. She bit her lip, looked away, then back again. "Okay. But only if you do one thing for me first.''

"Name it.''

"Go to the nearest store and bring me back every ounce of chocolate you can find. I'm going to need it.'' Then she hitched up her skirt, climbed over the sill and disappeared back inside.

It took three Hershey's bars and a Hostess Ding Dong before Anita could look Luke in the eye. Wrappers were spread around her in a circle on the kitchen table, as if she was some sort of twisted chocolate sacrifice. Luke had insisted she put her feet up on a second chair while he poured two glasses of lemonade.

"Really, you don't have to pamper me," Anita said. "I'm not breakable."

"Pregnant women deserve to be pampered. Get it while the gettin's good, as my grandma used to say."

She grinned. "If you insist."

"I do." He refilled her glass and placed it before her, then took the seat opposite. "I want to apologize again for—"

"Don't." Anita put up a hand, realized she still held a square of chocolate in it, dropped the treat, then raised her palm again. "If you apologize one more time for kissing me, I'm going to start feeling like there's something wrong with me. I'm pregnant, Luke, not contagious."

"That's not it, Anita." He toyed with one of the wrappers, folding the silver foil in and over itself. "And it's not that I'm not attracted to you. I am. Very much." His gaze met hers. The thread between them snapped taut.

A nervous hiccup escaped her. "Yeah, I'm real attractive right now. About as sexy as Mount Everest."

He shook his head. "You don't see what I see." He hesitated, as if he was about to say something else. Anita waited. Hoped a little, if she was honest with herself.

A second ticked by. Another.

"You were right, you know. You do scare me." He grinned a little. "It's just been a while since I've dealt with a woman in any kind of romantic way."

He snorted. "Hell, pretty much any way at all." Luke tossed the piece of foil into the trash and crossed his hands in front of him. "Anyway, I didn't want to talk about that. What I wanted to do is offer you a job."

Not what she'd expected to hear him say. Not by a long shot. She blinked. "A job? But I'm not doing the marketing thing anymore."

"Not for my company. Mark and I are doing things on a much smaller scale now. Down the road, we might need some help, but for now…" He wrapped his hands around the glass. "I need help with Emily."

"Emily?" she repeated.

"I want you to work with her, to help her out."

"With her report?"

He shook his head. "Help her become my daughter again." The glass twirled beneath his fingers, the pale yellow lemonade a swirl. "You're the only person she's had a civil conversation with in months. She hasn't done any homework since school started a week ago. In the last school year, her grades hovered in the lower part of the alphabet." He took a breath. "I need you to help me get through to her."

Anita put up her hands. "She needs a therapist, not me. I don't know anything about kids."

"You were a kid once, right?"

"Well, of course I was, but—"

"That's good enough for me."

Anita shook her head. "I'm not qualified to help your daughter deal with her grief. I could say one wrong thing and upset her more."

"All you have to do is exactly what you did to-day."

"Which is?"

"Help her with her homework, praise her a little. She's on out-of-school suspension for the next few days because of the flamingo-hair thing. Not to mention her continued refusal to go along with the dress code. If she could get caught up, maybe even do well on a test or two, I'm hoping maybe—"

"A little success will turn her head and make her want more?"

"Yeah."

Anita got to her feet and placed her glass in the sink. "I don't know, Luke. I'm not trained in this. I could make things worse."

"Trust me. It could *not* get worse."

She turned. "That bad, huh?"

He sighed. "Emily hasn't been the same since Mary died. It's like she put up this huge wall and now refuses to take out even a single brick. I've tried, God knows, I've tried. I've talked to a lot of therapists in the last eighteen months."

Anita crossed her arms over her chest and leaned against the sink. "What did they say?"

"Two of them told me to medicate her. A third said it was just a phase." Luke picked up another wrapper and began folding it into neat squares. "I'm not going to dope up my daughter. And I know this is more than a preteen *phase*. She needs someone to talk to." He tossed the silver box he'd made across the table. "It's just not me."

Anita went to Luke and put a hand on his shoulder. "Luke, she loves you. She'll come around."

He shook his head. "Anita, you know me. I'm a

realist. None of that fantasy happy-ending stuff for me. I deal in facts and figures. Emily resents me for her mother's death, and she's shutting me out. I don't blame her. Hell, there are plenty of days I don't like my own company.''

She bent down, capturing his gaze with her own. In his depths of blue, she saw such raw hurt that it pained her. "You're doing the best you can. It's not like they give you a manual and say 'Here's what to do when you lose your spouse.'''

"You don't understand. There's more to it than that. Emily isn't even—'' He shook his head, as if he'd decided not to finish that sentence. "Emily's the most important thing in my life right now. I'm willing to do anything, hire anyone, if it means getting through to her before it's too late and—'' he paused, took a breath "—I've lost her for good.''

"It's not too late. She's going to be okay. You're both going to be okay.''

He snorted and looked away. "I don't know about that. I need your help, Anita. Will you take the job?''

She glanced at the pile of bills sitting on her kitchen table. They weren't going anywhere. Apparently the mouse didn't find paper appetizing.

"Anita,'' he continued, leaning forward as if he was afraid she was about to say no, "I'll pay you fifteen dollars an hour, if you think that's fair. That's what I paid her last tutor. If you could put in, say, four to six hours a day with her for the next few days, that should be enough to help her get caught up.''

"I don't feel right being paid to help you.''

"Just pretend it's a marketing job.'' He gave her

the grin, a sort of lopsided smile that asked her to trust him and humor him all at once. "You're trying to sell my daughter on being good again."

She laughed. "When you put it that way—"

"I'm irresistible?"

"Oh yeah," she said, making sure she kept her voice light, joking.

He was irresistible. Her reasons not to get involved and to keep her heart to herself had seemed so sensible five minutes ago, but now they'd had been turned upside down and inside out just by his grin.

Hormones. That was all.

She put out her hand. When they shook, a surge of warmth ran up her arm, zinging through her with a jolt. "Now I can afford more than canned ham for dinner. The mouse will be pleased."

"Are you okay financially?"

"I just had a freelancing job fall through, that's all. I'll bounce back. I always do." She patted her belly. "I bounce a little better with the extra padding."

He hadn't let go of her hand. "Anita, if you need anything—"

"I can take care of myself, Luke. I set out to do this on my own and I will."

"It's not a bad thing to ask for help, you know."

"And it's not a bad thing to kiss a friend, either."

Now he released her. He pulled back and glanced around the room, as if he was looking for an escape hatch. "I better fix that door before I leave. The, ah, sun's gone down and the humidity's dropped a bit, so I should be able to get it open." Luke stood. The chair let out a squeal when he pushed it back. "Let me just get my tools."

Anita retook her seat and put her feet back on the opposite chair. "I'll be right here."

His cobalt eyes locked with hers. "I know."

Anita reached for another Ding Dong. She was going to need serious chocolate fortification if she was working anywhere near Luke and those eyes.

Thank God for work. Luke immersed himself in his computer whenever Anita came over to tutor Emily. It was a lot easier to spend hours fiddling with computer code than it was to figure out what he'd been thinking when he'd offered her the job of helping Emily.

On Em's side, things were going wonderfully. She'd responded well to Anita's deft touch and in three days had already made up most of her missed work. Emily had even started to crack a smile when Anita arrived. The happy face had been such a shock, he'd thought about calling *Ripley's Believe It or Not*.

Luke's alcove off the kitchen had become a torture chamber. Anita kept wearing those damn skimpy sundresses with ribbons for straps. They looked ready to fall off with the least gust of wind. Much to his disappointment, there'd been little to no breeze all week.

The skirts seemed to get shorter every day, exposing a bit more of her legs and driving Luke a bit more insane. She often walked to the house, and her skin had taken on a deep tan that only accentuated the contrast between skin and clothing. Every time he saw her, there was something else to push him further over his libido's already narrow edge.

On Monday, she'd worn her hair in a ponytail that hung low against the back of her neck. The style made her look graceful, almost elegant and yet, at the same time, sexy as hell.

On Tuesday, she'd put on lipstick, a dark shade of cranberry that kept him so focused on her mouth, he'd burned his thumb taking a piece of toast out of the toaster.

On Wednesday, she'd gone and painted her finger-nails and toes the same devilish shade of red as her lips. He'd taken one look at her feet and gotten so distracted that he walked into a wall.

On Thursday, she wore strappy black sandals and a short black dress. With her red nails, red lips and hair loose around her shoulders, she looked like a Black Forest cherry cheesecake.

That had tested the limits of Luke's patience and self-restraint. He'd mumbled some excuse about needing computer paper and spent half his day in Lawford, buying office supplies he didn't need.

Among the gel pens and ink-jet cartridges all he saw was Anita. He'd been so preoccupied, he'd spent a hundred dollars and driven halfway home before realizing his bag held everything *but* paper.

By the time he came back, Anita had gone home. He wasn't disappointed. Not one bit.

Luke dumped the office supplies onto the kitchen table and plopped into a chair. Emily's pile of books and papers were spread across the surface.

Emily came into the kitchen, poured herself a glass

of milk and took a nonchalant stance against the wall. "In case you're checking up on me, yes, I am all caught up on my homework. And today was the last day of suspension. I'll be out of your hair tomorrow."

"That's great, Em." Luke flipped the cover of Emily's math book shut. "So…did Anita help you a lot?"

His daughter shrugged. The pink in her hair had faded, leaving her almost a strawberry blonde. "She didn't make me feel stupid like some teachers do."

"You're not stupid."

Emily rolled her eyes. "You have to say that. You're my dad."

"I wouldn't lie to you, Em. Especially not about something important like that." But even as he said the words, he cringed inside. He'd kept something from her all her life. His secret was one Emily never needed to find out. If she did, it would destroy their relationship, and he was all she had. He opted instead for a change of subject. "Did Anita say anything about…me?"

Okay, not exactly the change of subject he was looking for.

Emily wrinkled her nose. "Geez, Dad. Why would she do something like that?"

"Well, you know. We used to work together and—" Why was he saying all this to Emily? How desperate could he be? Trying to pry information out of his twelve-year-old daughter like some lovesick junior-high geek? He gestured toward the paper-clipped stack on the table. "Is that your report on Churchill?"

"Yeah."

He flipped through a couple pages. "Can I read it?"

"I guess." He started to read, and she let out a sigh. "You aren't gonna, like, mark it up or anything, are you?"

"Emily, I'm not that bad."

"Dad, you're the red-pen police. Anita already looked it over and said I did great on my own."

On the first page he saw a typo in the third paragraph. A missing comma in the next sentence. "She didn't correct your mistakes?"

"She said I'm smart enough to find my own mistakes. She gave me a checklist of things to look for. I've been going over it."

Emily's voice had taken on a defensive tone. Luke looked down at the typos, back at his daughter, considering. He itched to tell her about the mistake. Any other day, he would have.

But where had that gotten him? Every time he helped her with homework, it was a disaster. A battle worthy of inclusion in the history books she so despised reading.

Until Anita came along.

Maybe Anita held the key to communicating with Emily, to helping his daughter find her place in school, at home and in Luke's life. He hoped like hell she did.

He should ask if Anita had a checklist he could go by: Ten Things A Dad Should Never Say.

Luke flipped the paper shut. "I'm sure you're going to do great." He laid the report back on the table, then took a seat and gestured for Emily to do the same. "Instead of reading about it, why don't you tell me what you learned?"

"*Dad.*" Emily sat in the chair and crossed her arms. "I thought if I got all my work done, I could go over to Sarah's house and play with her new PlayStation." Sarah, who lived two doors down, had become Emily's best friend after they'd moved in last year. Except for a penchant for heavy mascara, there wasn't much about Sarah that Luke objected to.

"I was hoping we could talk."

Emily had slumped in the seat and was fiddling with an extra paper clip on the table. "Can I go to Sarah's? *Please?*"

She was beginning to get that hostage look about her. Where was Anita when he needed her? She'd know how to make this work. "Go ahead." He sighed. She was out the door before he could finish saying, "Be home in time for dinner."

If Anita had a single other option besides Luke, she would have run the other way. She was a thousand miles away from her closest friend, alone in a new town and now...

Homeless.

On Friday morning, she stood on Luke's doorstep and pushed the doorbell. The strains of "Hail, Hail, the Gang's All Here" pealed inside. There was a scuffle of voices and footsteps and then the door opened. "Anita!" Grace's face broke into a welcoming smile. "What a wonderful surprise to see you. If you're here to see Emily, she went back to school today, but she should be home this afternoon."

"Actually, I'm not here to see Emily." She swallowed her pride. It settled in a big lump in her stomach. "I'm here to see Luke."

The smile on Grace's face widened. "Well, that's also a wonderful surprise. Let me go get him. Come on in." She waved Anita into the house. "Watch out for the suitcases."

Anita looked down and saw a half-dozen pieces of luggage in various colors and sizes stacked against the wall. Was Luke leaving? Moving out?

"Hi." Luke stood in the doorway of the kitchen, in cutoff jeans and a white tank top. His legs and feet were bare, his dark hair still damp from the shower. He looked relaxed and as comfortable as an Egyptian-cotton robe, ready to wrap her in familiarity and take her away from the stresses of her day.

Not to mention he looked awfully sexy, too.

Anita stared, at a loss for both words and chocolate.

"Did you come to see Emily? She's gone to school." Everyone else had disappeared, leaving them alone in the hall. The short, narrow space seemed tighter and warmer than usual.

"I know. Your mom told me. I'm here to see you." She waved at the suitcases. "Are you going somewhere?"

The spaniels dashed by in a whirl of yips and tails on their way to the backyard.

"No, my parents are. It's their fortieth anniversary this year. They're leaving on a cruise. Ten days in Bermuda."

A vague memory of Grace mentioning a cruise at

dinner came back. She'd forgotten all about it. This threw a kink in her plans. A big kink.

"Ten days?"

"Yep. They've been looking forward to it for months."

"And you're going to stay here with Emily? Alone?"

"That's the plan." He cocked his head. "Why?"

"Uh…" She looked at the luggage again. "This really isn't the best time to ask you this, but…" She closed her eyes and blurted the words out. "I need a place to stay. My kitchen's toast."

"What? What happened?"

"The landlord tried to save a few bucks by hiring his cousin's kid to fix the wiring. Apparently the guy got his license off the back of a matchbook, because he did it all wrong. I blew a fuse when I tried to use the toaster and that set off a little chain reaction in the walls. It was pretty ugly."

He was down the hall and checking her over in a half second. "Are you okay? Did you get hurt? What about the baby?"

"I'm fine, Luke." She laughed. "But the kitchen needs an overhaul. All new wiring and walls. And the smell. Lord, it's awful." She wrinkled her nose. "I think even the mouse left."

"Then stay here. With us. That house should be condemned."

"I really shouldn't—"

He cocked his head and grinned at her. "Are you worried about me? Or you?"

"I'm not worried about myself. I'm perfectly capable of sharing a roof with a man."

"Good." His grin widened. Did he have to stand so close? She could see the faint tan line against his tank top and for some reason, that drove her mildly crazy with wanting to tease a finger along the edge of his shirt. "Wouldn't want you pawing me over the pancakes."

"No worries there." Her voice sounded a bit too bright. "I'm a scrambled eggs kind of girl anyway."

His gaze zeroed in on hers. "I'll keep that in mind."

Oh, boy. Maybe this was a mistake. Maybe she should find a hotel room. Or a cardboard box to live in for a while. Tough it out in her powerless, stinky rental house.

Or face the fact that, thus far, her new life was a complete mess and she'd have been better off staying in L.A. Alone. Putting Luke and every feeling he conjured up a thousand miles away.

Or…she could stay here for the next few days. Make Luke wear a sweater, then run to the Sav-A-Lot and buy everything that listed cocoa as an ingredient. How long could it take to fix her kitchen anyway?

Anita glanced at Luke, at that irresistible grin that had stayed in her mind the entire drive from L.A. to Mercy.

Probably just long enough for her to lose her heart.

Chapter Six

That afternoon, Luke's mother and father left for their cruise in a whirlwind of goodbyes, kisses and barking dogs. Anita had left for a couple of hours to gather her things, then she returned to unpack and settle into one of the spare bedrooms. Emily had come home for three seconds, then gone to Sarah's, a reward for bringing home her first B in a long time.

As the clock struck half past four, that left Luke and Anita.

Alone.

He should have been working on the software design for another new client Mark had landed the other day. An hour ago, he'd been entirely focused on that account and getting the product delivered on time. That was his business, after all. His livelihood. His—

Anita walked into the living room, and he forgot everything he'd learned past kindergarten. Clearly not a good time to be working.

"Are you all settled in Katie's room?" he asked. He'd taken what he hoped was a nonchalant position on the sofa.

She perched on the edge of the cranberry wing chair. "It didn't take long. All I had was a suitcase and my laptop. I left the mouse behind."

"Poor guy."

"He'll survive." Anita crossed her legs. Her abdomen had expanded more in the last few days and her skirt popped up a few inches with the movement. She shoved it down, but plenty of leg was left for his viewing pleasure.

Maybe he should move into her house, with the rodent and the fried walls. If he stayed here, he'd probably end up having a heart attack on the first day.

Talk about Emily, peanut butter, weed control. Anything but how gorgeous Anita looked and how she'd started consuming his every thought.

He cleared his throat. "I wanted to thank you and pay you for working with Emily this week," he said, getting up to hand her a check to pay her for her tutoring, then retaking his seat. "Emily got a B on her math test."

"She did? That's wonderful!"

"I could tell she was pleased, though she'd never admit it."

Anita laughed while she tucked the check into her pocket. "Yeah, that would be totally uncool."

He fingered the edge of the sofa. "You've been a great help."

"I didn't do much." Anita shrugged. "She's a smart kid."

"You got her to smile again. That's more than I've been able to do in eighteen months."

"Luke, you don't give yourself enough credit. You're a great dad."

"Not so great, Anita. I wasn't there much when she was little. I was always at work." He got to his feet and crossed to the fireplace. Nothing burned there now, it was just a large, black hole. In the winter, they'd light it again, but until then, the space seemed empty, cold. "I wish I could get those years back."

"You're here now."

"I might as well be invisible." He picked up a silver frame on the mantel, a picture of himself and Emily when she was three and riding her tricycle for the first time. She was beaming at Luke from under a big floppy sunhat. That day seemed a million years away. "We don't get along all that well, in case you haven't noticed."

"Give her a little time."

"I don't have time. She's twelve. In a few years, she'll be out of the house and in college. This is my last chance. If I don't connect with her now…"

She rose and was at his side in an instant. "We'll make it happen, between the tutoring and everything. Don't worry."

He'd heard the word *we*. Did she mean it? Or had it been a slip of the tongue? He replaced the picture on the wood surface and let out a sigh. "All I do is worry. I've got that down pat."

"Well, now you have someone to worry with you."

Luke turned, taking in Anita's dark chocolate gaze,

so full of concern. They'd been friends long before
there'd been anything else between them. He could
feel that foundation, like a concrete block he could
stand on in a sandy beach.

He never realized how much he'd come to rely on
her when she'd been in L.A. He'd missed her voice,
her friendship in the past eighteen months. She'd been
a big part of his life, a source of support when his
business was going down the tube. She'd always been
there to lend a hand or a listening ear.

But now there was something else. Another degree
to their relationship, as if these last few days had
painted it another color, a brighter tint. Taking them
from the pale yellow of friendship into something
hotly crimson.

He reached out and grasped her hand. He sought
only comfort. Or so he told himself.

Before he knew what he was doing, she was in his
arms. He'd meant only to hug her, but when he'd
caught that jasmine perfume and felt the warmth of
her against him, reason left his mind.

He lowered his mouth to hers. *"Anita,"* was all he
managed before he kissed her.

A week of longing, of watching her from across
the room and denying himself even the slightest
touch, erupted in his kiss. There was nothing halfway
about it. Anita hesitated for a fraction of a second,
then reached for him, too, her arms tightening around
him with a surprising strength.

He buried his fingers in her mahogany hair, tan-
gling them in the silky tresses and drawing her closer.
His fingers danced along her neck, a sensual massage

that mirrored what he would do if they were in a bedroom instead of standing beside his mother's fireplace.

He didn't think about her pregnancy. He didn't think about his responsibilities, his work. He stopped thinking about his daughter, due home any minute. For so long, Luke had been living his life for other people. A few minutes, that's all he wanted, for himself. To calm this aching, driving need rumbling inside him.

His hands traveled down, along her back, sweeping along the delicate curve of her buttocks, hitching up the soft cotton of her turquoise dress, then releasing it again and moving to the front, to capture her breasts in his palms. Beneath his hands, he could feel the fullness of her, the added size brought on by her pregnancy. He drew his thumbs over the centers; her nipples peaked through the fabric in response.

Anita groaned and pressed to him, inflaming a fire that didn't need additional stoking. A train roared through his veins, driving him forward, propelling his need for her.

Never had he felt this heady rush of desire, so powerful it threatened to make him insane with need. Never had he felt this kind of want, stronger than a twenty-mule team tugging at him, urging him further.

He reached around her, pulling her closer, his mouth opening wider, wanting, begging for more. His tongue darted in, tasting the sweetness of her mouth. As if they didn't know where to go, his hands stroked here, there, everywhere, exploring the Anita he'd known for five years and yet never known. Not this way.

Too soon, too quickly, Anita cupped his face in her hands and took a step back. *"Luke."*

It took a few seconds for his brain to connect with his hands and his libido. He moved his hands to her waist and willed his erection to go away. Fast.

"This could easily go a lot further than either of us is ready for, you know."

The back of his mind was screaming for *further,* offering sacrifices if he'd satisfy even the tiniest needs. "You're right." He worked to get his breathing under control. "We should—"

"Stop."

"Yeah." *Damn.*

"If we're going to live together, even for a few days…"

"We can't be doing this." *Can we?*

"It's playing with fire."

He knew she was right. A week ago, he'd told her he had no interest in a relationship. He'd just made himself a liar.

He wanted her. He wanted to kiss her. Touch her. And yes, dammit all, make love to her until he forgot his own name.

He had never wanted anyone as he wanted Anita right now.

Not even his own wife.

"Dad! I'm home!"

Luke broke from Anita's grasp, just before Emily entered the living room, dumping her book bag on the floor.

"What's for dinner?" she asked.

"Hey, how about saying hello first?" Luke said.

Emily rolled her eyes. "Hi Dad, how was your day, now what's for dinner?"

Anita laughed, a shaky sound that told Luke she was a little unnerved by Emily's unexpected arrival. "I say we take this conversation into the kitchen. Then we can cover days and dinner all at once."

The three of them headed into the kitchen, quickly dividing up duties for an easy dinner of spaghetti. Emily set to work buttering some bread for garlic toast while Luke boiled water for the pasta. It was good to be busy, to be doing anything but staring at Anita and thinking about that kiss in the living room.

"How's Rocky doing?" Emily asked Anita.

Luke raised an eyebrow. "Rocky?"

"The baby, Dad. He's been kicking at Anita so much, I nicknamed him Rocky."

"Oh." He felt about as dense as the stainless-steel pot. "Yeah, they do that a lot about this time, don't they?"

"Geez, Dad, how long's it been for you?"

"This coming from the girl who just got a B in math?" He broke the noodles in half and dropped them into the boiling water. "I think you can figure that one out."

"Oh, yeah. Duh." She laid the bread on a cookie sheet and handed it to her father to broil.

Anita laughed and eased herself into the chair opposite Emily. "I've been feeling the kicks a bit more, lately. He's running out of room in there."

"Are you sure it's a he?" It was the first question

he'd asked about her baby, he realized. For the past couple of weeks, he'd been going along blithely, thinking only about himself and Emily, not thinking about Anita and the child she had on the way. He hadn't asked one question about how she was preparing for this baby—or if she was ready for the child to come. He didn't even know when she was due, for Pete's sake.

He might as well be living in a cloud for all he'd paid attention.

"I don't know. They told me at my last ultrasound that I could find out, but I'd rather be surprised. There aren't many surprises in life. I figure this one—" she laid her palms on her belly and a look of contentment came across her face "—is one of the best."

"I bet it's a boy," Emily pronounced. "My friend Sarah said there's this test you can do with a needle and thread to tell what the baby's going to be."

"Oh yeah? How's it work?"

"Let me get some thread and I'll show you." Emily scrambled to her feet and returned a moment later with a sewing kit. She threaded a needle, then suspended it over Anita's abdomen. "Sarah said if it goes back and forth, it's a girl. If the needle goes in a circle, it's a boy."

"Luke, come on over and see this. We need an impartial judge." Anita waved at him.

"I think it's going in a circle," Emily said.

Luke bent down and watched the needle. "I agree."

"That's two out of three. Sounds like a boy to me," Anita said.

Luke laughed. "Next you two will go into the tarot business together." He stood and thought how good it was to see his daughter smiling at him, enjoying herself. He gave Anita a smile that he hoped expressed his thanks for her inclusion of him in such a simple moment.

As they finished dinner preparations, the three of them settled into a comfortable silence, the kind that arose between people who'd known each other for years. Luke took a seat at the table and marveled again at how happy Emily looked.

"Well," Luke said, dishing up a plate for each of them. "What do you say we all take in a movie after dinner?"

Emily's eyes brightened, and Luke felt as he had when he'd hit his first home run in Little League. Emily loved movies. When she was little, her favorite thing had been her once-a-month trip to the Embassy Theater with Luke. Then the trips had stretched to once every other month and then once a quarter and then once a year and then...

He couldn't remember the last time he'd taken his daughter to a movie theater. How could all that time have gone by so quickly? How could he have missed it?

She opened her mouth, then paused, her face falling. "I almost forgot. There's this thing at school tonight. Just some stupid Back to School Night. Anyway, my teacher put something of mine up on the wall and..." She pushed her pasta around on her plate. "Never mind."

"Do you want me to go?"

She shrugged. "I think you're supposed to." She fished a paper out of her back pocket and handed it to him. "It says both parents should go."

"Oh, Em." Luke hated these moments, when Mary's death came rushing back and smacked them both in the face. When an idiotic paper from school had some insensitive reminder—a mother-daughter event, a family-tree activity. Just one more thing to remind Emily that her mother had died and her father wasn't doing a very good job of being a single dad.

"Since Mom is… I thought maybe…" She shoved some more spaghetti around, as if the words she was seeking were at the bottom of the pile. "Anita could go," she mumbled.

"You want Anita to go?" Luke handed the flyer to Anita.

"I just want her to, like, see my paper and stuff." Emily pushed back from the table. "Forget I asked. It was a stupid idea."

"I'd love to go, Emily." Anita laid a hand on the young girl's arm. "What about you? I see it says the students can come, too, and explain their work."

Emily shook her head. "Nah. I'm not very good at that stuff. I thought I'd just go to Sarah's."

"Oh, no fair. If I have to go back to school, so do you." Anita smiled. "We could all go out for an ice cream afterward. How's that sound?"

"Okay, I guess." But Emily's eyes were shining and a smile teased at the corners of her lips. "I gotta change first."

Emily was out of the room and back in a flash, wearing nice shorts and a matching T-shirt. She'd pulled her hair back into a neat ponytail and done her face with a light coat of makeup, topped with a dab of lip gloss.

This was the daughter Luke remembered—wholesome, sweet. He wanted to reach out, draw her to him, take in the scent of her hair, as if she'd still have that Baby Magic smell. He took a step forward, then dropped back. If he pushed her too far now, would she back away?

Emily helped clean up dinner without being told, then slipped on a pair of sneakers and dashed out to the car, taking the back seat.

"I think she's been taken over by an alien," Luke said to Anita from his view inside the house. "That whirlwind who ran by us is *not* my daughter."

"The real Emily was there all the time. She just needed a little coaxing."

"Well, whatever you've done is working. First her grades, now this. I think I need to nominate you for a Nobel Peace Prize."

"I wouldn't go that far." Anita bent over, trying to slip sandals onto her feet. "Oh geez, I can barely see my toes. This is so embarrassing. Luke, could you—"

"Certainly." He bent down and slipped the strap into the little buckle, securing it against her ankles. Her feet were pretty and delicate, the red polish a daring accent on slim toes. He fumbled with the latch on the second one, nearly locking his pinky in there instead of the strap.

How could a pair of feet be so distracting? And so damned sexy? His mind wandered back to the living room, to that kiss, to her breasts, to his hands on her breasts—

Finally, the shoes were on. Luke straightened and reached for his keys on the hook, turning away from Anita before she saw his testosterone set off a new record on the Richter scale.

He shouldn't get involved with Anita. Hadn't he learned his lesson already? Taking on another man's child would leave him on the outside, looking in, forever trying to get past the wall. He'd never feel a complete part of the child's life. He'd never be a part of the bond Anita and the baby had. He'd traveled that road once. Only an idiot drove in the wrong direction twice.

Mary had been so good with Emily, maybe too good. She'd built a special world for the two of them, one he'd never been invited into. If he dated Anita, and later married her, would that happen with her child, too?

Yet, a tiny part of him dared to hope Anita would be different. He'd already seen her make an effort to draw him in, to make him part of the triangle with Emily. And what he felt for Anita…

Well, it wasn't anything like what he'd felt for Mary.

"Luke? Is something wrong?"

"Huh? No, nothing's wrong."

"I know you. I can tell when something's bothering you. I'll pester you till you tell me what it is. So you might as well spill now."

"Nothing. Really."

She paused on the porch. "Do you want me to stay

behind? I didn't even think of that.'' She smacked her forehead. ''This should be your special time with Emily. I shouldn't intrude.''

''No, no that's not it at all.'' Luke swung around and heaved a sigh. ''Emily's reaching out, to both of us. To me, that's pretty much the equivalent of the Second Coming, so I'm going to do whatever it takes to make her happy. If she wants you along, I'm all for it. If she wants twenty sundaes at Sam's Sweet Scoop, I'm buying out the freezer case.'' Luke paused a few steps from the car, taking in his blond daughter waiting for him, an expectant half smile on her face. How long had he waited to see that sight? ''She means everything to me.''

''I know.'' Anita laid a hand on his shoulder.

He shook his head. ''You don't understand. Emily's special.''

''She's your daughter. I understand that.''

''It's more than that. She's—'' He cut himself off and looked down at the keys in his hand. ''She's going to be late if we don't leave now.''

''You can't bring that thing in here.'' The pimple-faced teen in the white triangle hat pointed at the door. ''You know better.''

Anita halted in the doorway of Sam's Sweet Scoop. The Back to School Night event had gone very well. Emily had shown off an A-minus on her Winston Churchill report, then taken them down the hall to see a detailed still life she'd done in art class. Most of her teachers had remarked on the change in her attitude and told Luke they saw great potential in her abilities. Now the three of them were waiting in line for an ice cream, the happy mood extending between them like a connecting thread.

"I said, you can't bring that thing in here."

Was the server talking to her? Her belly wasn't that big, was it?

Behind her, Anita heard a large "Garruf." Then panting. Either Luke had gone off the deep end or—

She pivoted. A massive Doberman stood behind her, tongue lolling. He appeared about as friendly as a wolverine.

"Meet Sweet Pea," Luke said with a grin. He gave the dog a wide berth and came to stand between Anita and the monstrous beast. "And Miss Tanner, her owner." He gestured toward a small, spry elderly lady who had a death grip on the dog's leash. "Miss Tanner, this is Anita Ricardo."

The woman scowled. "I know who she is. I know everything that happens in this town. It's about the size of a bread box. All you need to do is pay attention for half a second and you know the postmaster's son just ran off with the produce manager's daughter." Miss Tanner raised a thin arm toward the counter. "Now, are you going to stand there all day or are you going to let me and my baby get a banana split?"

"Ma'am, you can't bring a dog in here," the kid said, his voice rising and cracking in urgency.

"You tell him that, sonny, because my Sweet Pea wants an ice cream." Miss Tanner stepped forward. Her dog caught the scent of the sugary treats and took a giant lunging leap at the counter.

The kid backed up several steps, clearly more intent on seeing his sixteenth birthday than enforcing the health code. "Ah... How many scoops?"

"Three please. And a dish of cherry-chocolate crunch with nuts for me."

Anita bit back a laugh. In L.A., plenty of people had dogs and even indulged their pooches with silly outfits and special treats, but she'd never seen anyone take a Doberman into the neighborhood ice-cream parlor for dessert on a Friday night. Emily and Luke stood to the side, looking completely unconcerned, as if Miss Tanner did this every day. She probably did, Anita realized.

"Colleen, you really need to leave that beast at home," Miss Marchand said from the door. Outside, her dachshund sat tied to a lamppost, patient as a rock. "You know better."

"I'm old. People have to indulge me."

"You're not old. Just stubborn." Miss Marchand pressed a hand to her chest. "*I'm* old."

Miss Tanner waved her hand. "*Pshaw.*"

Miss Marchand rolled her eyes and turned to Anita. "I see you've met one of the nicer neighbors in town."

"Don't go telling people I'm nice," Miss Tanner interrupted. "You'll spoil my reputation. Who asked for new people to move into town anyway? Spoils the demographics."

"May I get you an ice-cream cone, Miss Marchand?" Luke inserted himself between the two women, clearly providing a change in subject. Miss Tanner snorted, yanked her desserts out of the boy's hands, and left. Sweet Pea trotted happily beside her, trying to snatch at the cone.

"Such a sweet boy," Miss Marchand said. "A dish of mocha, if you don't mind. I'll just settle myself at a table outside with my new neighbor." She linked her arm through Anita's.

"I'll bring you something, too," he told Anita, his face close to hers. She resisted the urge to lean against him and feel the warmth of his cheek. Ever since the living room, resisting Luke had become an exercise in futility. "I know your tastes already," he whispered. "Lots and lots of chocolate."

Anita could only smile. He'd mentioned chocolate in that deep, measured tone of his and her brain had melted right along with her resolve. She'd been trying to tell herself for the last two hours not to get too used to being with him, but, so far, it hadn't worked much better than the server's enforcement of the No Dogs Allowed rule.

Miss Marchand tugged on Anita's arm. They exited the ice-cream parlor and took a seat at a red-and-white-striped table outside. Now that the sun had gone down, the temperature had dropped, and a cooling breeze whispered past them, making the night comfortable. Light traffic hummed at a slow pace past them on Main Street.

Perfect, Anita thought. She leaned back in the wicker chair. Absolutely perfect.

Miss Marchand brought her dachshund over to sit beside her. "So, how do you like our town so far?"

"I love it." Anita glanced at the trees along the

sidewalks, the neat storefronts and strolling couples enjoying the evening air. "It's wonderful."

"Hmmph." Miss Tanner waved a spoon at her from the next table. "Next you'll be holding up the line at the Sav-A-Lot asking about the coupon policy. New people are a pain in the—"

"Colleen, eat your ice cream." Miss Marchand nodded at Luke inside the shop. "I see you found Luke."

"I needed to get my car fixed and—"

"He was handy. Not to mention as handsome as you remembered." Miss Marchand smiled. "I'm an old woman, not a stupid one."

"There's nothing between us. We're friends."

"Uh-huh. I've heard that before." Miss Marchand gave her dog a little pat. "Ask Luke what kind of 'friends' Mark and Claire are now."

"No, really. Luke and I aren't dating." And they wouldn't be, not if Anita could keep herself focused. She *knew* Luke. He was a good man, but also one who worked a million hours a week and kept his emotions close to his chest. She'd been deserted enough in her life. She wasn't about to set herself up for that again. Not on purpose.

"Why not?"

Anita smoothed her skirt against her lap. "It's complicated."

"It's the father of the baby, isn't it? He still coming around?" Miss Tanner dabbed at her lips with her napkin.

Miss Marchand turned toward Anita and cocked

her head, waiting for her answer. It seemed as if every table on the patio got silent.

"No. There is no father of the baby. Well, there is, but not…" Anita let out a sigh. "It's complicated."

"You young people. When I was your age, things were black and white."

Miss Marchand cast her friend a look. "Don't throw stones, Colleen."

Miss Tanner went back to her ice cream. Sweet Pea licked the last drops of her banana split off the sidewalk and settled onto her paws. She let out a loud belch, then yawned.

"Luke's a good man," Miss Marchand said. "Whatever—" she waved her hand toward Anita's belly "—*complications* you have going on, I hope you keep Luke's heart in mind. He's not up to being hurt."

"I'd never hurt Luke."

"I hope not. You seem like a really nice girl, but you have to understand, this is a small town. We look out for our own. It can take a long time to go from being outside to being inside, if you know what I mean."

She should have expected that. It was the wagon train, circling around to keep out the invading army. They weren't going to welcome her with open arms, not until she'd proved herself. "I'll keep that in mind, Miss Marchand."

Sweet Pea started to snore. Miss Tanner leaned in toward their table. "Tuesday is triple-coupon day," she said. "You remember that, and we'll get along just fine."

Chapter Seven

"**Y**ou don't have to do this, you know." Anita shifted against Luke. No matter how hard she tried, she couldn't find the perfect spot.

"This isn't exactly something you can do alone." He spread his legs wider. She wriggled into the extra space, settling against the softness of his golf shirt and shorts. Ah, there it was. Total comfort.

Sort of. Anytime she was close to Luke, comfort wasn't the word she'd use to describe how she felt. Distracted, hot, longing for more of what she'd tasted that Friday afternoon—

Hoo boy. Was she going to need more chocolate. Maybe the hospital sold it in IV form.

She'd vowed to stay away from him, even told herself a dozen times this morning that she wasn't going to ask him to come to class with her, but then, somehow, the words had slipped out anyway, sometime between "Will you pass the cream?" and "I'll have another helping of eggs."

She really needed to get a Ho Ho.

"I could get another partner," she said. "You probably have better things to do than—"

"Will you just shut up and breathe?"

She laughed. "You like being in charge, don't you?"

He placed his hands on either side of her abdomen. His palms were warm through the cotton of her dress. "I'm good at it."

She laid her hands on top of his and tilted her head back. From this angle, he looked stronger, broader. Depending on him wasn't such a bad thing. It was only for a couple of hours. Just a Tuesday night labor-and-delivery class at the Lawford City Hospital. "I'm better at being the leader, you know."

"Breathe," he ordered.

She huffed in and puffed out. Huffed in, puffed out.

"Are you focusing on your focal point?"

"I don't have a focal point."

"You better find one. Or Jan will be mighty disappointed in you."

Jan, the childbirth-class instructor, had so much energy and enthusiasm she sounded as if she took hits from a helium balloon during class breaks. Twenty minutes ago, Jan had entered the room singing "Oh What a Beautiful Morning" as a way to begin the class. She'd then launched into the tale of the delightful, nearly painless births of her five children.

Now she had six couples on the floor, breathing in

tandem while she darted from pair to pair, like a hummingbird on steroids.

"That's exactly right, Steve and Barbara!" Jan said to the couple on Anita's right. The duo had about as much enthusiasm for the class as a toddler going for a measles shot. They'd quit doing the breathing exercise halfway through. Now the husband sat beside his platinum-blond wife, his face a mottled red of exasperation. "You're doing a wonderful job!" Jan said, pumping a fist in the air. "Keep right on breathing!"

"I can't," Barbara whined. She made a sour face and let out a moan, then clutched at her stomach. "Ouch. I think I'm in labor."

Jan waved a hand at her. "Those are just Braxton Hicks. Totally normal. When you're in labor, honey, you'll know it. It'll be beautiful. Such a miracle." Jan clasped a hand to her chest.

"It's gonna hurt," Barbara said. "When do I get the drugs?"

"Drugs? You don't need drugs. The breathing will help—"

"I want drugs and I'm gonna have drugs." Barbara's mascara-coated eyes narrowed. She stared at Jan, as if daring her to disagree. "Okay?"

Jan shrugged. "It's always the mother's choice, of course. But let's practice the breathing. Just in case." She backed away from Barbara and hunkered down beside Anita and Luke. "You two must be so excited about your baby."

"Uh, this isn't—" Anita began.

"We are," Luke finished. "Very much."

Anita cast him a look. What was he doing? If he kept on saying things like that, the whole town would think this was his child. That would set off a problem Anita didn't need.

"Now, do you have your focal point?"

"I haven't come up with one. Nothing really appeals to me."

"Well, I have one for you. It always works in a pinch." She winked, then crooked a finger at Luke. He came out from around Anita and sat in front of her. "Look here," Jan said, pointing at his eyes. "Don't take your gaze off of him."

"Uh, okay." Not a hardship.

"Now, breathe."

Anita breathed in. Out. Looked at Luke, thought about that kiss outside her house, then the unfinished one in the living room yesterday and the simmering tension that had been running between them ever since.

Breathe in, breathe out, think of Luke, look at Luke—

"Whoa, Nellie! You keep breathing like that and you're going to have this kid right here on the floor," Jan said. "Relax, honey. This isn't a race."

Anita felt her face heat up. "Oh, sure. Maybe I should use a different focal point. Like something…plainer." Yeah, like a dish towel.

"I've got something for you." Luke reached into his pocket and withdrew something small, round and plastic. "Remember this?" He dropped a watch into her palm.

"You kept it?" Elmer Fudd's clueless face stared

back at her from under a plaid flannel hunting cap. Twin rifles ticked around his face.

"Of course I did. You gave it to me."

She remembered the day, more than a year ago. The morning after that steamy, senseless kiss in his office. A silly gift for his birthday, which seemed so stupid in the light of day, after the night that she hadn't expected. "As a joke. I didn't think you'd actually use it."

He shrugged. "I kept it as a reminder."

"A reminder?" She pressed the button on the left side and Elmer sputtered, "Be vewy, vewy quiet. I'm hunting wabbits." She laughed. "That I had trouble pronouncing my *R's?*"

"No." He took the watch face from her and traced the outer circle with his thumb. "To lighten up once in a while. Laugh a little. Live a lot."

"Did it work?"

He grinned. "Only when I remembered to use it for a focal point."

"Kinda hard to do when it's in your pocket."

"Exactly."

She took the watch from him and placed it on her belly. "There, now we can both look at Elmer and remember to laugh through the hard parts."

He grinned. "Sounds like a plan."

She arched her back and rubbed at a sore spot. "Just remind me I said that when I'm screaming for an epidural." In an instant, Luke was behind her again, settling into the comfortable place, his hand replacing hers and hitting the painful nerve with the exact right amount of pressure. "Oh, that's perfect. You are so wonderful at this."

"We make a pretty good team."

He'd said "we."

A little thrill ran through her. Fear or happiness, she wasn't sure. Two letters out of the alphabet and here she was, thinking about a future...

And worrying that he'd meant it at the same time.

Two letters. Nothing to get all worked up about.

"Okay, class," Jan said, stepping to the front of the room and clapping her hands to get their attention, "let's watch a little movie about the beauty of birth."

"I think I saw this one in sixth grade," some guy in the back piped up.

"This one is a bit different from the puberty primer you saw in junior high." Jan pushed Play on the VCR, then moved out of the way and dimmed the lights.

Images of pregnant women, expectant fathers and the beginnings of the birthing process popped onto the thirty-five-inch screen. In color. With sound.

"Oh, my lord," Anita said. She pressed a hand to her mouth. They hadn't covered *that* in sixth grade.

"Doesn't, ah, leave much to the imagination, does it?" Luke's voice held a mixture of surprise and alarm.

"No." She grimaced. "Any chance those are stunt doubles?"

Jan stood against the wall, a rapt look on her face, the same expression some women had on their wedding day. The other couples all looked as if they were sitting through a screening of a horror movie.

"Who *does* that?" Anita whispered to Luke when the scene switched to one inside the delivery room. "And naked, too?"

"Well, they were naked when they got this way. Might as well finish it up naked. Sort of brings the whole thing full circle."

Anita smacked his arm. "Only a guy would think that."

"Can you blame me?"

The tape continued, tracing the entire birthing process. In excruciating detail. "Ewww. Did you see that? How'd they even get a camera in there?" She shut her eyes. "Tell me when that part's over."

"I can't. I'm not looking, either."

She laughed, still in the dark. "Didn't you see all this with Emily's birth?"

"I missed the good parts. I got caught up in traffic. Mary had Emily before I could get there."

Anita peeked one eye open. "Okay, it's safe to look again. Nothing gruesome. Just a bunch of breasts."

"Good. My favorite part."

She smacked him again. Harder. "You're supposed to be concentrating on me."

"I am," he whispered in her ear. "Very much so." Her heart went to full tilt. There went her breathing again.

She took a breath in. Let it out. In. Out. Think about anything but Luke. She thought of chocolate. Nope, that led to thoughts of Luke.

Elmer Fudd.

Back to Luke again.

Impossible. With the man a centimeter away, his legs wrapped around her and his chest serving as a human pillow, thinking of anything but Luke wasn't going to work.

Why had she asked him to be her labor coach? Why hadn't she just asked...

Who? Miss Marchand? Sweet Pea?

She had no one here in Mercy. No one to call when the plumbing broke or the car died or she went into labor. No one but Luke.

She'd vowed to do this on her own, relying on no one. And here she was, doing exactly the opposite.

The video came to an end, complete with the happy couple holding a gurgling baby on a swing, the requisite setting sun behind them. There was a swell of orchestral music, then a cluster of doves flew across the screen.

"Oh, geez, that part gets me every time," Jan said. She swiped a hand across her eyes and pushed Stop on the VCR. "Makes me want to have another one."

"I want a lot of drugs and a C-section," Barbara said. "And I'm not having my baby naked in a hot tub with four of my closest friends shouting 'you can do it.'"

"Gee, Barbara, I thought that looked kind of interesting," Steve said. His wife shot him a look that would have fried an egg. He shrugged and returned to rubbing her back.

Jan handed out pamphlets on breathing techniques as the moms and dads gathered up their things and headed for the door. "See you next week! And remember the three Bs, dads. Back rubs, Breathing and

B vitamins! We need to take care of our mommies so they can take good care of our babies.''

The men headed out behind their wives. Luke walked beside Anita, the last pair to leave the room. When they reached the glass doors that led to the parking lot, he stopped, placing a hand over hers before she could press the handle. His palm was warm, so much larger than hers. She noticed the definition in his hand, the way the lines of his fingers showed the wear of a man who had a few years on him.

She decided she liked that. And that, Anita realized, was a very dangerous thing. She needed to pull back, step on the brakes—

"Want to go get some pie?"

"Pie?" There went her resolve again. He was right behind her, speaking the magic word, wearing that teasing, tempting grin.

"Wouldn't want Jan thinking I'm falling down on my coach duties. Gotta keep this mommy well nourished.''

Anita laughed. "Pie isn't exactly packed with vitamins.''

"Hey, it has most of the four food groups in it.''

She shouldn't go. She knew where it would lead. In a few days, Luke would go back to being Luke— buried in work, distant, busy, and she'd be alone. If she was smart, she'd skip the pie *and* the heartache.

"There's this café downtown," he continued, "and they make the best apple pie you've ever tasted. Marge, the owner, bakes it herself. Nothing out of a can, nothing from a freezer.''

"Homemade?" Temptation, thy name is apple pie.

"Absolutely."

His breath was warm on her neck, his hand still holding hers. A simple slice of pie. Nothing more. Yet, even as she agreed, she knew she was fooling herself.

Nothing about Luke, or about her relationship with Luke, had ever been simple. A taste of apples and cinnamon could become the tinderbox for the inferno she'd been trying very hard not to ignite all day.

Luke had noticed a gradual shifting in Anita's demeanor in the last two days. Ever since the kiss in the living room, things between them had been unbalanced, as if they were pulling on opposite ends of the same string.

He'd vowed to keep his distance after kissing her. But then there'd been the Back to School Night and the ice creams with Emily. She'd been there on Saturday morning, making pancakes in a robe that was too short and covered with flour.

She'd been everywhere. In his house, in his kitchen.

In his every thought.

Now she sat at an outside table at Marge's Diner, her dark brown hair lifting a little in the slight breeze. She was leaning back in the chair, her eyes closed, a look of such complete serenity on her face that he hated to disturb her, even for pie.

"You're much too pretty to bother," he said softly.

Anita opened her eyes. "You must be talking to another girl. Did you notice I'm twenty-five pounds overweight?"

"For a good reason." He didn't tell her that the added weight had softened her, filling out her curves in a way that made her seem more womanly, more Anita than ever before. Somehow, there didn't seem to be a polite way to say that.

She straightened. "Did you bring my pie?"

He laughed. "Of course. I can't shirk my duties as labor coach." He laid the plate before her and took the seat opposite with his own dish.

She picked up the fork, hovered over the plate. "You don't have to do this, Luke. I can find someone else to help me with the classes. Or, I can do it alone."

"I want to help you, Anita."

She shook her head. "It just complicates things between us."

His gaze met hers. "Yeah, it does."

He was beyond complicated. He knew, just by looking into her eyes, that the minute she'd walked back into his life, he'd been forced to face the truth he'd been trying to avoid since their first kiss eighteen months ago.

He'd never been in love with his wife.

His marriage had been a sham.

No one knew the truth about his relationship with Mary. And no one ever would. The cost would be too high to Emily and that was a price Luke couldn't afford to pay. Every time he was around Anita, his heart flipped in ways it had never flipped before and he knew...

He *knew*.

"You're right," he told her. "Besides, you're—" He waved toward her abdomen.

"I'm what?"

"Carrying another man's baby." Luke cut off a piece of pie, stabbed it with the fork, but left it on the plate. "You could get back together with the father. I'm probably intruding."

Anita ate a scoop of apple. "That's never going to happen."

"Don't rule that out, Anita. Every child needs a mother and a father. If there's any possibility—"

"There isn't, trust me." Anita ran a finger along the rim of her water glass. "He doesn't even know."

Luke paused. "You didn't tell him?"

"I, ah, went to a bank."

"What'd you do, date a teller?"

She let out a short burst of laughter. "Not a *bank* bank. A sperm bank. As in give them some money and get a baby."

"You...you..." He paused, trying to get his mind around what she'd said. "You paid to get pregnant on your own? What about that guy you were dating when I left?" He remembered how jealous he'd been, seeing them together, the summer before he moved to Mercy, knowing that he had no claim on Anita. After all, Luke had been the one to tell her to move on, that he wasn't ready for a relationship.

"Nicholas? It was one of those stupid leap-without-looking things. You know, lose your head and your heart. All the stuff they warn you about in 'Dear Abby.'" She let out a short, bitter laugh. "I don't know what I was thinking. I barely knew him. I guess

I was just trying to make up for—'' She looked away, then back. "Anyway, we ended up getting engaged. He broke it off as soon as I mentioned the word 'children.' They'd cramp his style, he told me.'' She shrugged. "I was the idiot. I should have known better. Depending on other people for your happiness just leaves you disappointed.''

"Not always.''

"I disagree.'' The way she said it told him the subject was closed.

Luke laid his fork down on his plate. "So you set out to be a single mother? On purpose?''

"Well, when you put it that way…''

"It sounds selfish.''

"Gee, thanks, Luke.''

"I didn't mean that. I just—'' He let out a sigh. "I know how hard it is to raise a child alone and I can't imagine *choosing* to do it. Why?''

"I've always wanted a family. I hadn't met anyone else who wanted one, too. Not to mention, someone I could love. That whole happily-ever-after thing.'' Anita took a sip of water, then replaced the glass on the table. "This seemed the easiest way.''

"You're happy with this decision?''

"I'm hungry right now. Let's have pie, not examine my life choices, okay?''

"But—''

"But five minutes ago you and I decided we shouldn't get involved romantically.'' Anita lopped off a chunk of pie with her fork, then popped it into her mouth. She chewed, swallowed, then waved the fork to punctuate her sentence. "And just so you know, I am happy. Very happy."

He looked at her. "This child will be growing up without a father."

"I grew up without a father. I'm not an ax murderer." She pushed the plate away. "Listen, I know the two-parent family is the ideal. But it didn't work out that way for me. And I'm okay with that. Who says I can't make it work? Who says I can't work at home, raise my baby, have a mouse for a pet." She smiled the Anita smile he had come to know as well as the back of his hand. "And live happily-ever-after?"

"Anita, it doesn't work that way, you—"

"Luke, don't say it. I love this baby, more than I ever thought it was possible to love anything, and the baby isn't even born yet. I've changed my entire life. With no doubts, no regrets, no reservations. I did it all by myself, without a husband. And I know, I feel it, right here," she pressed her palms to her abdomen and a soft, quiet smile came over her face, "that we're going to be okay."

Luke looked out across the town square, nearly empty now. A few night birds chirped their songs to each other. Anita was wrong. She had no idea how hard the road ahead would be.

How she would second-guess every decision, wishing she had a sounding board to help her make those choices on everything from schools to formula. How she'd want someone to share the heavy burden of shaping her child's life. How she'd worry that she would screw it up.

But how could he tell her that? Her face was bright, happy. Filled with expectations and hope. She rubbed at her belly in an absentminded circle, tracing the outline of the life inside.

He couldn't tell her about the sleepless nights that lay ahead, the heartbreaking choices she'd make, the ear infections and the school bullies, the fevers of 103 and the tests on fractions.

He couldn't sit here and preach to her about how she was doing her child, and herself, a disservice by going it alone. Because he'd unwittingly dumped all those things in Mary's lap, never knowing how heavy that burden had been...until he'd been left wearing Mary's shoes.

There was only one option.

Luke pushed his pie to the side and reached for both of Anita's hands, drawing them into his own. She blinked at him, startled by the suddenness of his movement.

He couldn't leave Anita to do this on her own. She needed him, whether she knew it or not. She needed him, and so did her baby.

He captured her gaze with his own, swallowed hard, then said, "Marry me."

Chapter Eight

For the seven hundredth time in the last twelve hours, Anita thought of last night. She'd walked away from Luke, leaving her pie and his marriage proposal, sitting on the table, both growing cold with each passing second.

She'd gone back to the house, packed her things and returned to her unfinished rental house. She didn't care if the repairs were done. All she needed was a place away from Luke. A place to think.

So far she'd done way too much of that.

He'd offered her that pity proposal, as if he thought she couldn't do this alone. The last thing she needed was a man who wanted to marry her because he felt sorry for her. *If* she ever married—and that was a big if—it would be for love. The kind of love a girl could depend on to be there through thick and thin, rain or shine, like some kind of mailman's creed.

Ha, as if that kind of love even existed.

"If you sweep that porch any harder, you're going to wear those floorboards clear through."

Anita jerked her head up. A young woman, not much older than herself, stood on the sidewalk, pushing a double stroller laden with bags and matching dark-haired toddlers. The twins sat inside, munching on bananas.

"I'm Katie Webster, Luke's younger sister." The young woman had a friendly smile and chestnut hair, pulled back in a dancing ponytail. She wore cutoffs that had painted kid handprints on each hip and a pink T-shirt with A Pair of Posies: Flowers to Make You Smile across the front.

"Hi!" Anita laid the broom against the house, then trotted down the stairs. She bent down and peered at the nearly identical cherubic faces inside the stroller. "What gorgeous kids!"

"They're a handful. Actually more than two handfuls." Katie laughed. "But I love them to pieces. Meet Gracie and Eddie."

One of the twins reached a chubby fist forward and bopped Anita on the nose, then giggled when Anita let out a playful beep. She felt a rush of anticipation for when her baby would be old enough to do that. "They're adorable." She straightened and put out her hand. "I'm forgetting my manners. I'm Anita Ricardo."

"I know. The whole town's abuzz about you."

"It is?"

Katie laughed. "Get used to it. Mercy's always looking for something to talk about and, right now, you and Luke are it."

Anita shook her head. "But there's nothing between Luke and me."

Katie raised an eyebrow. "That's not what they're saying down at Flo's Cut and Go. Those ladies practically have you two married off."

The words "married off" caused an odd twinge in Anita's stomach. "I think I need to sit down." She backed up and lowered herself onto the stoop.

"I don't blame you. Living in Mercy takes some getting used to."

"I thought it would be so…"

"Norman Rockwell-ish? Kind of like *It's a Wonderful Life*?"

"Yeah."

The little girl finished her banana and grabbed her brother's out of his hands. He let out a howl.

"Gracie, that wasn't nice." Katie reached down, tried to get the banana back, but Gracie was having none of that. Katie broke off a chunk of what was in Gracie's hands and handed it to the boy. He shoved it in his mouth and chewed through a smile. "Small-town life has its warts, just like anything else. But I wouldn't trade it." She fanned at her face with her hand. "Gosh, what a hot day. I hope this heat wave breaks soon."

Anita got to her feet. "Would you like to come in for a little while? Have some lemonade? I made cookies."

Katie glanced at the twins, now wrestling over a stuffed toy. "Do you have any precious valuables in your house? Antiques? Anything breakable? At all?"

Anita laughed. "I'm sure they'll be fine."

"Okay, but don't say I didn't warn you. They don't call them the Terrible Twos for nothing." Katie grabbed the bags from under the stroller and handed them to Anita. "You take these and I'll get the kids. I brought over some baby clothes—boy and girl just in case—a monitor, diaper bag, changing pad. Matt, my husband, will come by later with a baby swing and a playpen."

It was a generous gift. Anita blinked, unsure of what to say. "I can't thank you enough. I hadn't bought much of anything yet. But…are you sure you don't need any of it for another baby?"

Her new freelancing job search had paid off and she'd found a few magazines to work for. Plus, her first bootie order was on its way to Gena. She had money coming in, along with the money she'd earned from Luke, but she hadn't started baby shopping yet.

"Are you kidding me?" Katie dug in a zoo-patterned diaper bag and came up with a matching toy for the one the twins were scuffling over. She handed it to Gracie, cutting off a cry midscream. "I have two-year-old *twins*. I'm done having babies for a while. A long while. Matt says he wants to have five kids—no, Gracie, don't stick your finger in Eddie's eyes—I told him he can stay home and—Eddie, you can't eat your sister's hair—I'll go build houses all day. I think his job is the easy one. Eddie, I warned you—"

Anita bent toward the carriage. "Who wants some cookies?"

Two pairs of chubby hands went forward, reaching for Anita, the squabble forgotten. "Me! Me!"

"I think you've just been elected favorite aunt. By them and me." Katie undid the safety belts and helped the toddlers out. They scrambled up the stairs and had a grip on the door before the adults had reached the top step.

Anita waved Katie inside the house. "You'll have to excuse my kitchen. It's not quite finished yet."

Not quite finished was an understatement, Anita realized, looking at her house and seeing it as she imagined Katie would. The wiring was in and the wallboard was up, but that was about the extent of the renovation thus far. Any prettying up would have to happen later. Undoubtedly, she would have to find some place to stay while the rooms were being painted and plastered. She doubted the fumes would be good for her.

One place was out of the question. She thought of the quaint little house on Cherry Street, of the warm, raucous welcome she'd had that first night at the Doles' home, then quickly put it out of her mind.

She was done with Luke. For good.

She waved Katie into a seat, then headed over to the counter and poured her guest a glass of lemonade from the refrigerator. "Let me get the kids some cookies. I'm sure they've cooled by now."

"I can't believe you baked in this heat." Katie took a seat and wiped a hand across her forehead. "Either you have a big-time nesting instinct or I'd say you're trying to work one idiot Dole man out of your system."

Anita turned and got busy refilling the ice tray, then placing it in the freezer. "What makes you say that?"

"You have no doors on your kitchen cabinets, yet your canned goods *and* your spices are alphabetized. You've got every cleaning product known to man out on the counter. Not to mention the way you were attacking that porch earlier."

Anita took a seat at the table. The twins dashed by, laughing and chasing after each other with cardboard tubes. They'd already forgotten about the cookies. "I guess I have been trying to keep busy."

She didn't mention the six pairs of booties she'd crocheted last night, working until her fingers couldn't move the crochet hook anymore. Every time she'd tried to close her eyes, Luke had been there. Every time she sat down, Luke's face was the first thing she thought of. If she paused to eat, she thought of Luke and the pie.

Thoughts of Luke wove through everything she did. The only solution had been activity. Cleaning, crocheting, writing, cooking. Anything and everything.

And not a single thing had worked.

"You've got it bad." Katie laid a hand on Anita's.

"Is it that obvious?"

"Trust me, Luke's worse."

Anita snorted. "I find that hard to believe."

"My brother is a moron, but he's also a heartbroken moron. I don't know what he was thinking about, proposing to you like that."

"You know about his proposal?"

Katie laughed. "Nothing stays a secret long in our family. If you're going to be a part of it, you better learn that early on."

Anita shook her head. "I moved to Mercy to start my own life, not to horn in on someone else's. I want to do this on my own, without relying on anyone else. I don't want to marry Luke. I don't want to be a part of your family." She put a hand to her mouth, then added, "I'm sorry, I didn't mean—"

"I know. You don't need to apologize. You're about to be a mom and you don't want an instant set of buttinskies telling you what to do. I understand that." She paused, wagged a finger at the twins. "Gracie, don't smack your brother in the head."

Anita rose, retrieved the container of cookies, dispensed one to each of the twins, then returned to the table and offered one to Katie, who thanked her and took one. "I really like your family. But sometimes it's weird being among so many people."

"Did you grow up with a lot of brothers and sisters?"

"Sort of, but none of them were mine." Anita took her seat again. "I was an only child. I never knew my dad and my mom died when I was ten. I was a foster kid, you know, going from house to house."

Katie put a hand to her mouth. "That's awful."

"It's okay. I turned out all right." An odd tightness filled Anita's throat when Katie reached out a hand and clasped hers. Lord, her pregnancy had her all emotional. Why else would she get upset talking about her past? Normally, it didn't bother her that much. She cleared her throat. "So, how's Emily?"

Katie smiled, as if she understood Anita's need for a change of subject. "Not speaking to Luke, but okay. She thinks he did something to drive you away."

"I should talk to her. Explain that it was me, not him."

"No, you shouldn't." Katie took a bite of her cookie and swallowed before continuing. "My brother is a great guy but he has all the communication skills of an orangutan. He needs to learn how to confront what's going on in order to solve the problems. With Emily." She leaned forward, a caring smile on her face. "And with you."

Eddie came tearing into the room. "Gwacie hit me!"

"See what you get to look forward to?" Katie smiled. "Actually they're wonderful. Especially when they're asleep."

Both of Katie's children had dark, almost ebony hair that curled at the ends. Anita found herself wondering what her child would look like, whether her baby would favor her, or the unnamed donor who had provided the other half of its life.

For a second, she felt a twinge of regret that she wouldn't be able to trace eyes and hair and hands, that she wouldn't have a husband to compare to her child.

No, she told herself. No regrets. She'd made this choice with her eyes open. "Do they look a lot like their father?" she asked.

"They're both the spitting image of their dad, but I think they have the personalities of my brothers." Katie laughed as she hefted Eddie into her arms. "Be nice to your sister, okay?" The little boy nodded, then squirmed away, his mind already on something else. "Hey, I have an idea. Next Wednesday night is movie night on the town lawn. They always play an old favorite. I think this month it's *From Here to Eternity*. Everyone brings a blanket and a picnic. It's hokey, but it's a lot of fun. Do you want to go with Matt, the kids and me?''

"Hokey is perfect," Anita said. It would get her out of this house. Away from thinking about Luke. Save her from wearing the floorboards—and the broom—down to splinters. "I'd love to go."

"Great. We can pick you up around seven. Bring some more cookies and you'll win Matt over instantly."

"Deal."

Katie rose. "I better get the kids home. If they don't take a nap, they'll be hell on wheels later." She covered her mouth, stifling a yawn. "Actually, I think I need the nap more than they do."

Anita helped her get the reluctant toddlers back out the door and settled into the stroller, using cookies as bait. "It was really nice to meet you. Thanks so much for all the baby stuff."

Katie laid a hand on Anita's arm. "You know, you're in this family now, whether you and Luke stay together or not."

"But—"

"We all sort of adopted you. My mom, me. Emily." Katie smiled and released Anita. "Besides, we needed somebody to inherit all these baby clothes. When we get Nate settled down, then you'll have someone to pass them on to. He's the only Dole left standing in bachelorhood." She gave Anita a wink, then said a quick goodbye and left, pushing the stroller. Gracie and Eddie waved chocolate-covered hands.

Anita headed back into her house. She picked up the broom, but didn't sweep. She watched the retreating figure of Luke's sister and wondered about what she'd said. About the family "adopting" Anita. About them welcoming her as one of their own.

And most of all she wondered about Luke missing her as much as she missed him.

She should be trying to distance herself, to pull back. All her instincts told her to do that before she got hurt. But her heart…

Her heart wasn't listening this time.

"Hey Luke, how's that software coming?" Mark's voice carried clear and confident across the phone line from California to Indiana. It was Thursday, two days after Anita had walked out on him. He'd been sitting in his office chair for two hours, accomplishing pretty much nothing all day. "It's not like you to be late on anything. Usually you're early, you big overachiever."

Luke leaned back in his chair, ignoring the protesting squeak of the wood. "I've, ah, been a little tied up with things."

"Like Anita?"

"How'd you know about her?"

Mark chuckled. "The Dole family party line. Mom told Katie, Katie told Claire, who told me. I'm glad to hear it, bro. You deserve some happiness."

Luke snorted. "I wouldn't call myself happy right

now.'' In fact, since Anita had walked out on his proposal, he'd been miserable.

"Flip the glass around. It's half full, not half empty.''

"There's more to it than that.'' He let out a breath. "Anita's pregnant.''

"Yeah, I heard. It's not…'' Mark didn't finish.

"No, it's not my baby. She went to one of those do-it-yourself places and well, did it herself.''

Mark chuckled. "That is such an Anita kind of thing to do. She's one determined lady. Good for her.''

"What do you mean, good for her? She's pregnant and alone and—''

"And she's not Mary, Luke. This isn't a rerun of your life.''

Luke popped forward in his chair. The air in the room seemed to grow still, silent. "You know about that?''

"I'm your twin. I know everything.''

"But…how?''

"I put some pieces together, that's all. I can add, too, you know.''

"Oh.'' Luke felt like smacking himself upside the head. He and Mary had married quickly, but there had been enough of a discrepancy in the dates that someone could have figured it out. "Did you ever say anything to anyone?''

"Nope. Not my job. I leave the telling to you. It's your life.''

Luke let out a sigh that didn't feel the least bit like relief. "Even Emily doesn't know.''

"You, ah, think that's wise?"

"At the time, it seemed the best decision, but now…" Luke toyed with the papers by his desk, stacking them into a pile that didn't need rearranging. "I don't know. She's twelve."

"She's pretty mature."

"She's been through a lot in the past eighteen months."

"You gotta let her grow up sometime." Mark paused. "And you have to let go and start over sometime, too."

"I have started over. I'm living my life."

"Uh-huh."

"What's that supposed to mean?"

"Nothing. Just uh-huh."

"That's what I thought." Luke reached for his project planner and flipped forward a couple of pages until he got to his notes from his last conversation with Mark. "Now, back to the program for the client. I had a couple of questions."

"Down to business already?"

"That's what you called about, isn't it?"

"I called to check up on you." The concern in his brother's voice was clear, despite the hundreds of miles separating them.

"I'm fine," Luke insisted. "And if you'll tell me what I need to know, I can get back to work and then you can get this project delivered to the client. Then everyone's happy."

Mark let out a chuff of disagreement. "Okay, but on one condition."

"What?"

"You don't bury yourself so far into this project that you ignore the hot, sexy brunette who lives just a couple of streets away. Don't brush me off about this, either. You have a chance at true love. Don't let it slip out of your hands."

"Mark—"

"I can hear the *but* in your voice. Don't even say it. What you had with Mary was good, but it wasn't…well it wasn't everything love can be. I know, I can hear you laughing on the other end. I'm probably the last guy you expected to hear this from."

Luke chuckled. "You were a confirmed bachelor not so long ago."

"Meeting Claire changed everything for me. I've seen you with Anita. Before we left L.A., there was something between you two. Something that doesn't come along every day. Take a chance, Luke."

"She hates me right now."

"Nah, she doesn't hate you. She's mad at you. *That* you can change, trust me. Romance the girl. Every woman likes a little romance."

"All right, you win. I'll send her some flowers, serenade her with a harmonica on the back porch."

Mark laughed. "I'm not sure about the harmonica."

"Hey, it's been a while for me. I'm not exactly a dating king like you," Luke said.

"You'll figure it out. Just go with your gut."

"Sounds like a plan." Luke leaned back in his chair. "Now, can we get back to the software program?"

For the next hour, they talked about the project, the

specifics of what the client wanted and how Luke was going to take the client's dream and put it on a computer. Luke promised to have a preliminary program by the end of the week.

He hung up the phone, booted up his computer and set to work. He should feel recharged. Excited about the new challenge. On any other day, work gave him satisfaction. Instead he felt as if he was missing something by being here in the alcove instead of—

Instead of where?

He knew where he wanted to be. With Anita. But he'd already screwed that up.

What had he been thinking, proposing to her like that?

If he'd been her, he'd have walked out on him, too. He'd behaved like an idiot. He didn't blame her for moving out and going back to the half-finished rental house.

Why had he proposed? At first, he'd told himself it was for her child, so the baby would grow up with two parents instead of one, but he knew he was fooling himself. He'd known Anita for the five years they'd worked together and had felt more than friendly feelings for her for a long time.

Longer than he'd like to admit.

Longer than he'd ever admitted to himself. Or to her.

In fact, he was...

Luke got to his feet, pushing the chair back in a sudden swift movement that sent the maple seat skittering across the vinyl flooring. He paced the kitchen, filled with a surge of unspent energy. From the window, he crossed to the doorway. Then to the sink, where he poured a glass of water that he forgot to drink.

He paused at the window, his gaze on the vast expanse of green in the backyard. The swing set that Katie's twins loved when they came over to play. The tree he and Mark had hung from when they were little. Emily's bike, forgotten outside and lying against the base of the oak. This was his home, his life.

And for the first time ever, it all looked a little brighter. Sweeter. Because of Anita. Mark's words rang in his head. And the pieces finally fell into place.

"I'll be damned," he said to himself. "I'm falling in love with her."

Now he just had to figure out what the hell to do about it.

Chapter Nine

"Breathe in, breathe out. Focus. Think of your happy place," Jan said to the class.

"My happy place is a Jacuzzi," Barbara snapped. "With a big margarita."

"Alcohol and pregnancy don't make a good mix." Jan made a little frown at her uncooperative student.

Anita squirmed against the pillows she'd brought, trying to get comfortable. A stack of fiberfill pillows wasn't quite the same thing as having Luke behind her. She'd come to the second class alone. Telling him she could take care of herself and then calling him to come to Lamaze class with her was not a smart idea, to say the least.

If she could just get comfortable, she'd be fine.

Yeah, right, said the little voice in the back of her head. She wasn't fine at all.

She wriggled and twisted, stuffing one of the pillows under one hip. Jan crossed to the VCR, another tape in her hand. The class let out a collective groan. Anita arched her back and rubbed at the ache just above her right hip.

"Here, let me get that." Luke's voice, warm and soothing, in her ear. His hand, even warmer and more soothing, against the painful spot.

She jerked forward. "What are you doing here?"

"Being your coach. Now breathe. And focus."

"But—"

"But nothing. I said I would be. Just because we had a disagreement doesn't mean I reneged on that."

"I told you I wouldn't marry you. That's more than a disagreement."

Luke grinned and Anita got the feeling he had something up his sleeve, some plan she wasn't privy to. She'd been resisting him for the past week. Ignoring the flowers. Refusing to answer his phone calls. Doing her best to give him the message that a relationship was out of the question. "A minor setback. I don't hear you breathing."

She huffed and puffed a few times. "Setback for what? There's nothing to setback from."

"Turn around and focus on the video," he said. "I think Jan is putting in the sequel."

"I'm not watching. I can only imagine what part two is going to be like."

"I intend to watch and take notes. It might come in handy later."

She turned around again. "What are you talking about? Didn't you hear me say no? I'm not marrying you, Luke. I don't need a knight in shining armor. I can take care of myself."

"I know that. I'm not trying to rescue you." He leaned forward, his mouth next to her ear. "Just romance you."

She gulped. "Romance me?"

"Yep. I'm going to sweep you off your feet, Anita Ricardo."

"Why?"

"If you have to ask, then maybe your hormones are making you blind." He brushed a kiss against her ear, then leaned back, acting as innocent as could be.

The movie started. Jan dimmed the lights. A darn good thing, because Anita's face felt hot, and emotions were pinging through her heart like errant sonar. Just when she thought she had Luke Dole and her life all figured out—

He went and turned it all upside down.

What on earth was he doing?

Kissing her. Romancing her. Teasing her.

She had to try to keep her head on straight. With Nicholas, she'd moved too fast and then been burned when it turned out he'd been the exact opposite of the kind of man she'd needed.

She tried to move forward, inching away from Luke, but he kept her against him, settling her into that comfortable spot as if he had some instinctual knowledge of where her body fit best against his. Comfort infused her, easing the aches and pains of her pregnancy. She gave up the battle between her head and her heart and relaxed against him.

A few minutes couldn't hurt. Could it?

Jan's movie pick today was tame, a twenty-minute show-and-tell on infant first aid. Nothing gruesome, no naked screaming women. The tape wound to a close, and Jan turned the lights back on. "Okay, class!" She clapped her hands together, her face bright and happy. "Tonight, we're going to try something a little different. One of the things the daddies must learn is to anticipate what the mommies need. Sometimes in the delivery room, the best communication is unspoken. Right now, we're going to work on our silent communication skills."

She waved the men around to sit facing the women and instructed the couples to hold hands. "Now, look deep into the eyes of the woman you love and tell her what she's thinking."

Luke came around to face Anita, spreading his legs so the two of them formed a kind of human triangle. He put out his hands and she slipped her palms into his. An instant zing of connection whizzed through her, a jolt of electricity that told Anita she was fooling herself.

She wanted Luke. Not just physically, but emotionally, too, as if he were a part of her. Some missing link that had yet to be filled in.

She caught her breath. Never had she felt like this before. Oh, boy, she was in trouble.

His deep cobalt eyes locked with hers. She couldn't have looked away if the Notre Dame Marching Band had come parading through the room. Everyone and everything dropped away. There was only Luke and a tightening, tensioning knot raveling between them.

"Tell her what she's thinking," Jan said, dimming the lights. "Really read your partner's mind." A slight murmur started up as the couples began talking.

"You want me," Luke said softly, "but you're afraid."

"I'm craving ice cream with pickles, not a man." Anita let out a nervous laugh.

"Don't joke about this, Anita. I'm serious." He squeezed her hands and inched forward. "If there's one thing Mary's death has taught me, it's that life is short. Don't let your best chance at love slip away because you're afraid to grab it."

"I'm not afraid of love."

"Oh yeah? Then why have you been avoiding me?"

"I'm not avoiding you."

"It's been a week since we saw each other. Did you get the flowers I sent?"

There'd been five bouquets, each delivered personally by Katie. "Yes. They were beautiful. I sent back a thank-you note with Katie."

"I don't want a thank-you delivered through my sister. I want to see you."

"You are seeing me. You're supposed to be reading my mind."

"I think I'm doing a pretty damn good job, too."

She let out a sigh. "You've got it all wrong."

He tugged her closer. "What do I have wrong? You aren't interested in me? Look me in the eye and deny it."

She met his gaze and opened her mouth. *Say it. Say the words that will end it now and Luke will go away. He's going to leave eventually,* she told herself. *Everyone does.*

She'd let herself get too close this time and now

she was going to get hurt if she didn't say the words
she had to say.

"I'm not interested in you, Luke."

"You're a terrible liar."

"What makes you think I'm lying?"

He released her hands and cradled her chin with
his palms. "Because I saw the tears in your eyes
when you said those words. I can tell you want to
kiss me by the way your mouth opens and closes and
your breathing kind of catches. And your hands trem-
ble when I touch you. I feel the same way, Anita. I
want to kiss you so bad, my heart aches like its being
squeezed. You can lie to yourself all you want, but
you can't lie to me." He trailed a hand along her jaw,
his eyes soft and kind, his voice a whisper. "I know
you too well, sweetheart."

"So! What'd you learn, daddies?" Jan's voice
jerked Anita away from Luke. She scrambled back
several feet, never so grateful for an interruption in
her life.

Her heart hammered at twice the normal rate.
Surely Luke and half the room could hear it racing.
She pressed a hand to her chest and pivoted away
from him, under the guise of following Jan as she
made her way around the room to talk to the other
couples.

"I learned Steve has all the ESP skills of a mon-
key," Barbara said. "I was thinking about a bubble
bath and a nice long nap and he was thinking about
sex, for God's sake. That is the *last* thing on my
mind."

"It's always the last thing on your mind," he muttered. "As soon as you said 'I do'—"

"Well, we'll just have to work on our communication skills, won't we?" Jan said brightly, then moved quickly on to the next couple. A moment later, she reached Luke and Anita. "So, what did you learn?"

"She needs a back rub and a piece of pie as soon as class is over," Luke said. He'd saved Anita from a response.

And damn the man, he'd read her mind, too.

It had taken a lot of talking, but he'd managed to get her to agree to some cookies from Marge's Diner. Anita had been adamant that it didn't mean anything, that he wasn't to take dessert as a symbol of anything more than a bunch of calories.

They had taken the cookies and walked down Main Street to the park. It was dark now, the town nearly silent. "Tell me about yourself," he said, gesturing toward a bench.

Anita took a seat, then reached into the bag and withdrew an oversize chocolate-chunk cookie. "What do you mean? You've known me for five years. You know everything there is to know about me."

"In the last few days, I haven't gotten a hell of a lot of work done." He settled beside her and waved off her offer of a cookie. "You want to know why?"

She took a bite of cookie, and he had to resist the urge to follow it with a kiss. "Okay, why?"

"Because I've done nothing but think about you.

I'm not normally a guy who spends his time day-dreaming.''

She blinked, clearly thinking about that. ''Yeah, that's true. I don't think I've ever seen you lost in thought.''

He leaned forward, trying to find the words that would tell her what he felt without scaring her half to death. There were so many thoughts in his mind, all pent up from the past few days, racing to get out. Ever since he'd realized his feelings, his chest had this odd tightness to it, as if he might burst if he kept all those feelings inside a minute longer. ''I'm a software developer. Your typical boring computer geek. My life has never been exciting. I've never leaped out of bed, raring to get at the day. I've never wasted two hours of my afternoon debating red roses over white chrysanthemums.''

''The mums won, didn't they?''

''I thought they'd be a little different.''

She took another bite of the cookie. ''I liked them.'' Her voice was quiet, almost shy.

''Good. I hoped you would.'' This was new ground with Anita. He didn't have the safety of a business relationship, or the tutoring of Emily to retreat to when things got too personal. Luke took a breath and moved forward. ''I haven't been working because I've been thinking about you. A lot. Wondering what your life was like when you were growing up. What your favorite color is. If you like cats or dogs. If you like pop music or rock and roll.'' He shrugged. ''Silly things, but at three in the morning, when all I can think about is you, they seem important.''

She had moved over an inch or two, an almost imperceptible distance, but enough to signal that he had said too much. "Luke, I—"

"Just start with the easy stuff. What's your favorite color?"

She bit her lip, looked away, then back at him. "Red."

"There, that wasn't so hard. Cats or dogs?"

"Cats. Dogs are a bit needier than I like."

"I'm a dog person myself." He grinned. "I think we can compromise."

Anita got to her feet and crossed to the playground a few feet away. She hugged the slim metal pole of the swing sets. "Luke, this is crazy. I'm not interested in a relationship with you. I'm here to raise my baby. Not to re-create the perfect household. That's not me."

"Why?" He swung around the pole, taking her free hand in his. "I think you're lying to yourself. Or at least to me. Why can't that be you?"

She let out a laugh. "It's a fairy tale. It doesn't happen." She tried to tug her hand away, but his grip remained firm.

"What happened to you, Anita? What happened in your life to make you think you don't deserve happiness?"

Tears welled up in her eyes but she swiped them away with the back of her fist. "Nothing. I just know the realities of life. You can't depend on anyone but yourself. So don't try to convince me 'happily-ever-after' is anything more than a lie concocted by the brothers Grimm to sell a bunch of books."

"Was Nicholas that bad?"

Anita jerked away from Luke and the pole and sat down in one of the swings. She pushed off with her toe, rocking back and forth over the sandy base. "I was stupid when I met him. I rushed into things, lost my head. Later, I found out that he wasn't who I thought he was. At least I woke up before I married him."

"So you admit to some spontaneity in romance?"

"It only happened because I was trying to get over—" She cut herself off and looked away.

"Get over what?"

"Nothing."

"I don't have to be in the CIA to know you're lying to me. Tell me. Get over what?" When she didn't answer, his memory started running through some dates. When she'd met Nicholas. The surprise of how quickly she'd become engaged to him. He came around in front of her and stopped the swing. "Were you trying to get over…me?"

Anita ran a hand through her hair. "I thought we were out for a walk and some cookies. Nothing more."

"I was an idiot that night," he said. "I kissed you and then I got scared. I said some things that—" Lightbulbs exploded in his brain. No wonder women thought men were stupid. It had taken him eighteen months to put the pieces together. "I told you not to count on me. That I wasn't in a position to give you anything in return."

"And that you were leaving, moving back to Indiana.'' She hauled herself out of the swing and brushed past him. "It's old history, Luke. Let it go."

"Anita, things have changed now. I'm different. You're different."

She spun around. "Are you? Tell me something, Luke. How different do you think you are? I worked with you for five years. I got to know you pretty well. I haven't seen a huge change in you since I moved here."

"Maybe you haven't been looking very hard."

"You're standing here, trying to get me to face some truths about my life. Why not face your own? Why did you have to hire somebody to get through to your daughter? She's not all that difficult to get to know. You've just never gotten close to her. Why?"

It was his turn to walk away. She'd hit his sore spot, the one area no one had ever questioned. Except him. He crossed to the slide, running his hand along the metal. "There are things you don't know, Anita."

"There you go, being a turtle again. You retreat, Luke. Into work or whatever. You pull back and you leave. Maybe not physically. Maybe it's just to that little alcove in the kitchen, but you're gone. I'm through with people who leave me." She pressed the bag of cookies into his hands and then leaned forward and laid a quick, soft kiss against his cheek. "I'm not strong enough for that. I'm sorry."

Then she turned on her heel and left.

Chapter Ten

"This isn't going to work," Matt Webster said. He had one squirming twin on his knee, another had already escaped, Katie in hot pursuit. "They have no interest in movies that don't come with animated blue dogs."

"I remember my mother telling me I was quite the hellion when I was little." Anita patted her belly. "I figure I'll be in for some revenge soon." She settled herself carefully on the blanket, propping against a pillow she'd brought. Several dozen families were already set up around them. A few dogs ran in a circle in the corner of the park, nipping at each other's tails. A big screen had been set up at one end of the open area and a popcorn stand to the right of that. The smell of the freshly popped corn wafted across the park.

She forced a smile to her face, trying to pretend she was enjoying herself. Ever since her conversation here with Luke last night, she'd been feeling miserable. Being in the same spot again twenty-four hours later wasn't helping her mood.

Had she gone too far? Said too much? She'd touched a nerve when she'd hit on his relationship with his daughter, she'd seen that in his eyes. The last thing she wanted to do was hurt Luke.

Oh, Lord, she'd really screwed this up. Now she'd lost a friend and something much more, but she couldn't think about that, or she'd surely break in two right here on the Mercy Town Lawn.

"Hey, isn't that Luke over there?" Matt gestured to Gracie. She perked up in his arms and waved a chubby fist toward "Uncle Wookie."

Anita told herself she wasn't going to look. That she didn't care. That she could live in this town with him and not have her heart skip a beat every time he happened to be near.

Liar.

A few feet away, Luke was shaking out a green plaid blanket and setting it up for himself and Emily. He had a cooler and a couple of bags of food from a fast-food place. Emily looked a little reluctant to be there, yet excited at the same time. She sat down far enough away from her father to register some teenage rebellion but close enough to show she didn't hate him, either.

Anita shifted and leaned back on her elbows. She shouldn't care if Luke was there.

She shouldn't care that he hadn't once looked in her direction. That he hadn't appeared to notice she was here. That he hadn't even said hello.

"Don't hit him. He didn't do anything to you," Matt said to his daughter.

"They missed their nap," Katie explained, carrying a reluctant Eddie back to the red-and-white Indiana University blanket. She gave him a juice cup, which he promptly tossed away in favor of a chocolate chip cookie. She let out a tired sigh. "I missed mine, too."

A butterfly fluttered in front of them. In a flash, Gracie was out of Matt's grip and dashing after it. Eddie tried to scramble after his sister, but Katie maintained her grip on him. He flailed his arms and cried. "Look, Eddie, the movie's on," Katie said.

That only made him cry more.

Matt returned with Gracie, swinging her in his arms, butterfly forgotten. As soon as he got near the blanket, though, she started to shriek. Katie threw up her hands. "Okay, I'm ready to admit defeat. This was a bad idea."

"Until they put dancing animals on the screen, I think the kids aren't going to be interested in the movie." Matt grabbed a toy out of the diaper bag and handed it to Gracie, but she only batted it away. "Maybe we should take them home."

"I feel so bad." Katie turned to Anita, trying to hold a conversation over Eddie's bobbing head. "I invite you out and now I desert you."

"I don't mind. I can stay and watch."

"Are you sure? I hate to leave you here."

"My house is only a couple blocks away. It's a beautiful night. I'm having a great time."

"Well, if you need anything—" Katie looked over

in Luke's direction, but left the rest of her sentence unsaid. Gracie slipped out of Matt's hands and dashed toward the swing sets. "Okay, that's my cue. I better go before Gracie makes it to Albuquerque. I'll call you tomorrow. We can do coffee again."

"I'd like that."

A few minutes later, Katie, Matt and the twins were gone in a flurry of kids and baby bags. Anita laughed, watching the parents try to keep up with the toddlers. She settled back on the blanket and watched the world of 1940s Hawaii unfold on the big screen in front of her.

But she didn't see Montgomery Clift's face on the screen. She saw Luke's. It wasn't the screen star she saw kissing Deborah Kerr. It was Luke she saw. Kissing her own lips. Anita rolled onto her side and glanced at him.

He was staring at her, his clear blue gaze so intent he seemed to be a statue. She felt her face heat up and, at the same time, both of them looked away. Then back, then away, like shy teenagers.

This was ridiculous. Why should she care? She'd told him she didn't need him. She didn't want a relationship with him.

If that was so, then why did she feel such a twinge of loss? And why did her blanket feel so vast and empty?

Luke hadn't heard one word of the movie. If someone had asked him what was playing, he doubted he could have said if the film was black-and-white or color. All he'd noticed from the second he'd flung out the blanket on the ground had been Anita, sitting a few feet away under an elm tree, pretty as a painting.

"Dad, this is *so* boring," Emily said. "Who wants to see two dead people kissing?"

"Those people aren't dead."

"They are now. What's this movie, like a hundred years old?" Emily shifted and toyed with the candy bar beside her. "When you said movie, I thought you meant the new Jet Li film. Not the movies in the park."

She said the last as if it was a case of the plague. "You used to love coming here."

"When I was, like, five. I'm not a kid anymore."

He sighed. "No, you're not."

"Hey, Em." A lanky teenage boy with hair that reached past his shoulders came over and stood by their blanket. "Whatcha doing here?"

"Nothin'." She leaned back, looking more bored than she had five minutes ago, if that was possible. Luke noticed she distanced herself from him, too, as if trying to pretend she wasn't anywhere near her father.

"There's a party over at Lisa's tonight. You should come."

"Really?" Emily's eyes brightened, then she shrugged, affecting nonchalance. "Yeah, sure. I might."

Over Luke's dead body. No way was his daughter going anywhere with a boy who wore earrings in layers.

"Cool. See ya, dude." He tossed a half wave Luke's way, then shuffled off.

"Before you even ask the question, the answer is no. That kid has all the ambition of a tree sloth. Don't even think about hooking up with people like that."

"Dad! Do you even know who that was?"

"Justin Timberlake?"

"Eww, gross. No. Only Kevin Lewis, the cutest guy in school. I cannot believe he talked to me! *And* asked me to a party. I want to go."

"I said no."

"Dad, you are ruining my life."

"There will be other parties, trust me."

Emily slumped against the blanket. "Not with Kevin."

"Yes, with Kevin. Now watch the movie."

Emily seemed to settle in and, for a minute, she watched the film. Luke's attention wandered. Out of the corner of his eye, he saw Katie and Matt put the twins into the stroller and exit the park, leaving Anita alone.

Maybe he should invite her over. Ask her to join them. Share the blanket.

Duh. Yeah, that would go over well. Gee, Anita, I blew the marriage proposal, totally screwed up a simple walk in the park…want to share my blanket?

Mark had advised him to romance Anita. Easier said than done. He'd dated a few girls in high school, married Mary right after graduation. His twelve-year-old daughter probably had more dating experience than he did.

Speaking of which, Anita had been right. Maybe it was time he came clean with Emily. Maybe telling the truth would finally break down that barrier between them. Had he been setting up a wall all these years and blaming Mary? Instead of himself?

He glanced at Emily. Now was certainly not the time to tell her. Soon, he promised himself. Soon.

He leaned back on his elbows and looked over at Anita. She glanced away quickly, as if he'd caught her gazing at him. Hmm…seemed she was more interested than she was admitting.

He got to his feet. "I'll be right back," he told Emily. Then he crossed to Anita's blanket.

She sat up straighter. "Luke! Hi. I, ah, didn't know you were coming here tonight."

"It's been a long time since I took my daughter out to a movie. This probably wasn't the best first choice because she thinks it's the most boring movie in the world, but—" he shrugged "—I tried."

"You get an A for effort," she said. "And trying is important, too."

"Could you sit down?" a woman behind him said. "We're trying to watch the movie."

Anita moved to the left, making room in her blanket. She patted the space beside her.

"Are you sure? Last time I saw you, you didn't seem to want to share much of anything with me."

She shrugged. "It's only for a minute. You probably want to get back to Emily soon, right?"

"Oh, yeah." He kept his disappointment from showing as he sat down beside her. "You made cookies?"

"Chocolate cravings." She smiled, an almost shy grin. Since when had Anita ever been shy?

Dare he hope *he* was the reason behind this new

side to her? Had his presence affected her more than
she'd let on?

"Double chocolate, my favorite."

"I know." She toyed with the silky edging on the
blanket. "I mean, you mentioned it in the diner yesterday. I was baking and wanted cookies and...well,
they sounded good."

Way to cover up, he thought. Sounded as if he'd
been on her mind today. Luke took a bite of cookie
and allowed himself a small measure of hope that
Anita might be returning his feelings, whether she
knew it or not.

Dark clouds skittered across the moon above them.
Humidity hung low and heavy in the air. It looked
like rain. Luke hoped the storm would hold off until
later. He didn't want anything to spoil this détente
between them.

"I'm sorry about last night," he said. "I was out
of line, intruding in your life like that."

Anita cocked her head and her dark hair tumbled
over her bare shoulders like a wavy waterfall. The
contrast against her white sundress had the startling
effect of night and day, yin and yang, angel and devil.
His fingers itched to reach out and touch those tendrils, to draw her nearer to him, but he knew already
that if he pushed too hard, she'd only back away. "It
was partly my fault, too. I got too defensive. Whenever people get too close, my first instinct is always
to run."

He chuckled.

"What?"

"I was just thinking. You called me a turtle. I guess

if I'm a turtle, that makes you a hare. You run, I hide in my shell.''

She leaned back on her elbows and laughed softly. "We're quite the pair, aren't we?"

"Oh yeah. A match made in heaven." He rolled on his side and waved the cookie at her. "They say opposites attract."

Anita looked up at the moon and let out a breath. "I don't think attraction's ever been the problem between us."

"No, it hasn't."

Just then, the skies opened up, the summer rainstorm coming hard and fast, ending Luke's plans for a nice evening with Anita. Families scrambled, gathering up blankets, coolers and kids, dashing for their cars.

Anita got to her feet, Luke's hand at her elbow to help her up. She grabbed the blanket.

"You stay under the tree," he said. "I'll get Emily and our stuff and then drive you home."

"Okay." She hugged her back against the tree trunk, seeking as much cover as possible.

Luke dashed off, dodging the rain and the running people. He found his blanket, his food...but no daughter. He cupped a hand over his eyes and scanned the area around him. "Emily?" He pivoted, looked some more. *"Emily!"*

He jogged a few feet forward, called her name again. Ran to the right, to the left, called again and again. No sign of Emily anywhere.

"Do you see her?" Anita stood at his side, holding the square of blanket over her head.

"What are you doing?"

"Helping you look for Emily."

He sighed. "We're not going to be able to find her in this mess. Let's get dried off and look for her when it stops raining." The rain was sluicing down on them now. "You head for the tree, it's the closest. I'll grab my stuff, then we'll go for the pavilion."

Anita made a mad dash toward the tree, still holding the blanket. The sodden material started to slip in her fingers, the edge dangling by her sandals. Luke watched Anita fall, like a movie happening in slow motion. She tripped over the lagging hem of the blanket and tumbled onto the sidewalk edge.

He sprinted forward and reached her a second later. She looked like a puddle of white on the concrete. "Anita! Are you all right?"

"I...I think so."

He scooped her up and carried her the few feet to the tree. "Are you sure? Is the baby okay?"

"I think it's just my leg."

He glanced down her left leg and saw a large gash and a growing bump that seemed to be getting wider and uglier by the second. "We should call the paramedics."

"It's not that bad."

"Yes it is, trust me." Luke glanced up but the park was empty.

"Is there even a fire department in a town this size?"

"Just a volunteer force, but I bet the guys were on call tonight because of the movie." Luke pointed toward a building about twenty feet away. "Do you think you're up to being carried over to the pavilion? There's a pay phone over there and I can call for help.''

''Luke, I can take care of—''

''Don't even tell me you can take care of yourself this time.'' He chuckled. ''You definitely need to rely on me for once.''

She looked at her knee, then at him. ''You're right.''

''You need to say that more often.'' He bent over and scooped her into his arms.

''Don't get used to it.''

As soon as Anita was in Luke's arms, she knew she should have chosen to hobble on her injured leg instead. She was playing with far more dangerous and breakable parts of her body by being this close to him.

The rain had begun to taper off to a slow drizzle. Luke stayed hunched over Anita and kept her close to his chest and the softness of his T-shirt. It was warm there, comforting, and very, very enticing.

Luke was right about her. She was a hare, running from everything that scared her. She'd learned to keep a step ahead of attachment. To leave a relationship before it got too involved.

And like the hare in the fable, she was tired. Tired of acting as if she had it all under control.

Anita leaned against Luke's chest. Her knee throbbed. She allowed him to carry her, to shoulder her burden. She let herself be comforted by him. Just this once.

They reached the pavilion too fast. Before she knew it, he had laid her on a picnic table as gently as if he were handling a china doll. "Stay here. I'll call for help. Are you okay?"

"Yep. I'm holding up just fine."

"Tough cookie, aren't you?"

She grinned. "I don't crumble easily."

"That is one bad pun."

"Hey, I never said I was a comedian."

He leaned over and pressed a kiss to her lips. "I'll be right back. Don't miss me. Too much."

She did miss him, she realized, as soon as his mouth left hers. Her heart did a funny flip-flop and her pulse raced at double speed. When he left the room, the empty feeling quadrupled, as if he'd taken part of her with him.

That scared her to no end. She didn't want to care about Luke. She didn't want to fall in love with him—

Fall in love? Where had that come from? There was no way she was falling in love with Luke. No way at all. She'd been very careful to keep her feelings to herself, to step back when things got too close. To stop herself from—

Or had she?

Oh, this was bad, very bad. Loving someone led to the ultimate hurt. Loving someone left her vulnerable. Open to pain, disappointment. Like a wound that never healed. She had to turn those feelings off. Now. Before she got in too deep.

When Luke came back a few minutes later, his blue eyes connecting with hers, that lopsided grin on his face, those hands reaching for her in friendship, concern and something more, she knew she was fooling herself.

There was no going back. She wasn't going to be able to forget him. To dismiss the way she felt. Her heart, it seemed, had moved forward, even while her head told her to stay back.

"We're in luck," he said, totally unaware of the emotional battle waging inside Anita. "I ran into George, one of the volunteer firefighters, outside. He has his radio on him and he called the EMTs. They should be here in a couple of minutes."

"Great." She raised her leg onto the table, which eased the throbbing a bit. "Well, I guess you can go now. I'm sure you want to go look for Emily."

"She's gone to a party with Kevin, the earring boy wonder."

"Kevin?"

Luke grimaced. "According to Em, he's also the cutest boy to walk the planet. To me, he's every father's worst nightmare. Hair down to here—" he touched a hand to his bicep "—and more earrings than brains."

Anita chuckled. "I can see why he'd bother you."

"He invited her to a party at some girl's house. Mercy's a small town, but not so small that I know where every teenager named Lisa lives." He spun around, peering past the columns of the pavilion. "Maybe I should ask George if he knows where these kids might be."

"If you want to go, Luke, go. I can take care of myself."

He turned back to her and the look in his eyes

caused everything inside her to become a senseless puddle. "No, you can't. Not all the time. Even Snow White had to ask the dwarfs for help once in a while."

"She was a cartoon."

"A damn good-looking cartoon at that."

"And I'm not?"

"You, honey, are the most beautiful woman I have ever seen. Snow White doesn't even compare to you."

She shook her head. "What were you drinking from that cooler?"

"Iced tea. Not even spiked." He stepped forward, so close she could see the dark lashes that framed his eyes, feel the heat emanating from his skin. "Since the first minute I saw you, I thought you were beautiful. And ever since you came to Mercy...well, I've seen you with new eyes. Beautiful doesn't even begin to describe you anymore."

"*This* is not the Luke I remember. You never talked like this before."

He took her hands in his. Warmth and something more, something almost electric, hummed between his touch and her palms. "I never had a reason to before. I've never felt this way about anyone. Ever. I mean, it probably sounds like a cliché, but now I wake up happy. I go to sleep happy. I damn near sing my way through my day, even after we've had a disagreement." He drew her closer to him, placing her hands on his chest. She could feel the steady thump-thump of his heart against her knuckles. "I've fallen in love with you, Anita. Completely, totally in love."

Anita opened her mouth, shut it. She sat there, stunned. "In…in love? With me?"

Her pulse rocketed upward. He was in love with her?

But…but was it real? Or was this just an extension of his marriage proposal? One step further in his pity for soon-to-be-single mom Anita?

Or maybe, her heart dared to interject, he was being real.

He grinned. "You're surprised?"

"Stunned. Shocked. Yeah, I'd say surprised."

"Why? You're not unlovable, you know."

She turned away, bit her lip. Words had left her, as if they'd drained away with the last bits of the rain.

She was saved from responding by the appearance of the EMTs. Two men, one tall and thin, the other short and wide, entered the pavilion, each carrying a medical case. "Hey, Luke, how are ya?" the tall man said.

"Just fine, Ted." The two exchanged some small talk as the EMTs got their cases opened and set up. "That's a nasty gash you have there, Miss Ricardo," he said to Anita.

"You know my name?"

"This is Mercy, ma'am."

She chuckled. "I should have known."

Ted cleaned the wound, then wrapped her knee in gauze. "That should do you. Be sure to stay off your feet for a while and use some ice to keep the swelling down. And, you'll probably want to keep someone nearby to fetch things for you, help you get around the house.'' He directed a pointed glance toward Luke.

"Should she go to the hospital?" Luke asked. He'd hovered nearby the entire time.

"If you have any pains or bleeding, anything out of the ordinary, you should go," Ted told her. "The damage seems to be all in that knee, though, and it should be healed up in a few days. Just keep this guy around. He's good for that kind of thing." Ted gave Luke a playful jab in the shoulder.

"I'm good for a lot of things," Luke said, his mouth close to Anita's ear.

My Lord, if he keeps this up, I'll be putty in his hands.

Anita had the distinct feeling that an injured knee was the least of her worries.

Luke carried a protesting Anita out to the car, drove her the few blocks to her house, then carried her up the steps and inside. He opened the door with one hand, then toted her to the couch and laid her carefully on the cushions, grabbing some pillows to prop up her head and her injured leg.

Once she was settled, Luke took a seat in the space beside her. "When I saw you fall today, I almost had a heart attack."

"Because of losing Mary?"

"No, that was different." He looked down into his lap, clasped his hands. If he had any hope of Anita letting him into her heart, he knew he better start by letting her into his. That was where he'd gone wrong all his life. Anita had been right about him—he'd been the one who built walls, not Mary and Emily. It was time those walls began to come down, by telling the truth. "I was never in love with Mary."

"But…but I thought…"

"Everyone did. We made a good go of it. We had the best intentions, we really did." He draped his arm across her and over the back of the couch. "It's ironic, the way she died, given the way shc and I came together."

"What happened?"

"She was late picking up Emily from school. Got tied up at the grocery store or the dry cleaners. I don't know. I was at work. Of course. That was my life. Work and more work."

"You put in a lot of hours in those years. I remember I'd drive by your office on my way home and see the light still on. I'd wonder sometimes when, or if, you ever left."

Luke ran a hand through his hair. "Too late, Anita. I was always too late." He swallowed, then continued. "You know how the traffic can get in L.A. You leave one minute late and suddenly you're caught in a twenty-minute jam. Plus it was raining that day so the roads were a mess. Mary was turning too fast onto the street that led to Emily's school. Some guy who'd lost his job and spent the afternoon feeling bad for himself in a bar was coming the other way." Luke closed his eyes, for a brief, horrible second seeing the whole scene again—the yellow police tape, the crumpled van, the quiet, still ambulance, the policemen shaking their heads. "He didn't see the stop sign. He didn't see my wife's van."

"Oh, God, Luke, I'm so sorry."

"They say she died right away. She didn't feel a thing. I have that at least." He swiped a hand across his face, rubbing at his temples. A dull throbbing had begun in the forefront of his head.

He took a breath, then went on. "I didn't go back to the office that day. Or the next. Or the day after that. When I did return, I spent half the time there that I had before. Then the company tanked when the tech industry went under."

Luke shrugged, then went on. "You know what? I'm glad as hell. I needed that wake-up call. I moved back here, started something a lot smaller with Mark. I can work at home, work my own hours, see my daughter and eat dinner with her every day. Granted, she doesn't want me there most of the time, but I'm there anyway." He brushed a hand across the top of the sofa and when he spoke again, his voice had dropped several pitches. "Mary was always the one there with Emily when she was little. They were so close. They had this *bond*. Em and I never had that. I decided a year and a half ago that I had to do something to change that. My plan hasn't gone so well so far—" he let out a chuckle "—but I'm not giving up."

Anita studied him for a long, quiet moment. "You really have changed, haven't you?"

"More than you know. It's been a long eighteen months, Anita. I've done a lot of thinking. I'm still a little bit of a turtle—" at that, he grinned, and he saw her answering smile "—but I'm working on it."

She reached up and cupped his face. Luke thought

nothing could have felt sweeter in the entire world. "I guess I've been wrong about you."

"Not entirely."

"Enough." With one slow, seductive move, she brought her mouth to his.

Fireworks exploded in his brain. Anita held nothing back. Her fingers roamed through his hair, her lips explored every inch of his, taking, tasting, asking for more. He nibbled on her lower lip, teasing at her. She groaned and opened her mouth wide to his, her tongue darting in and begging him to return the favor.

There was a clatter from the other room. Luke jerked back. "What was that noise?"

"Probably the mouse, inviting over some friends," she murmured, her eyes half-closed. "He knows I baked cookies."

He kissed one lip, then the other. "Every bit of you is sweet, you know."

"I try." She wrapped her arms around his chest, tilting her head up under his.

"I don't think this is going to help your leg heal."

"Oh, I don't know about that. I forgot all about the pain." She smiled. "Maybe we should do it again."

He put up a finger. "I want to. Believe me. But I decided tonight to be honest with you and I haven't finished. Can I take a rain check for a few minutes?"

She paused, her gaze searching his. "This is something serious, isn't it?"

He nodded. "Yeah. There's something more I have to tell you. Something nobody knows, well, except for Mark, who figured it out on his own. I think if we're going to take this—" he laid a finger against her lips "—any further, then I need to be honest with you."

She laid back against the pillows. "Okay. Tell me."

Luke inhaled, held the breath, then let it out again. This was the hardest story to tell. If he wanted a real relationship with Anita, he needed to start it on a foundation of honesty. "The reason I never loved my wife is because…Emily isn't mine."

"What?"

"When I was in high school, my best friend, Jeremy, dated Mary. His parents hated her. She was from the wrong side of the tracks and they thought she'd just bring him down. He was a party guy, and he got really drunk one night. Typical teenage idiocy." Luke got to his feet and paced the room. "I tried to stop him from driving. Mary did, too, but he wouldn't listen to us. He got mad and took off in his car." Luke paused at the door, as if he could see his past in the glass panes.

"And he got into an accident?" Anita asked when he didn't finish.

"Yeah. He…didn't make it." He pivoted to face her. "Mary was only a few weeks pregnant. She tried to tell his parents, but they blamed her for Jeremy's death. They told her they never wanted to see her, or the baby, ever again, and they stuck to that all these years. The three of us had always hung out together— you know how it is with high-school kids. Sometimes you didn't know who was dating who because we were such close friends."

"So you stepped into Jeremy's shoes?"

Luke crossed to the couch and sank beside her. "Her parents were poor, they couldn't help. We were in high school, for God's sake. But it was more than that. Jeremy's baby was all either of us had left of him. We both loved him so much, and we knew we'd love the child." Luke paused, drew in a shuddering breath. His gaze searched hers, hoping she'd understand. How could he explain what he'd done? "He was my best friend," he said, his voice a shattered whisper. "What else could I do?"

"Not many men would do that, Luke."

He shook his head. "I don't know about that."

She took his face in her hands. "You are one in a million. I don't know if Emily knows how lucky—"

"How could you?" Emily's voice, high and shocked, came from behind them.

Luke jerked to his feet. "How'd you get in here?"

"I climbed in the window. One of the kids said some pregnant lady got hurt at the park. I figured it was Anita, so I thought I'd sneak in to check on her instead of making her get up to answer the door. But now I find out—" She cut herself off. "I can't believe you lied to me." Her voice cracked and a single tear slipped down her cheek.

Luke reached for her. "You don't understand, Emily."

"Oh, I understand everything, Dad. Or should I even call you Dad? And you two, kissing. I thought you cared about me." She spun on her heel and left the room.

"Emily!" Luke ran after her, but she ran faster.

* * *

Luke came back two and a half hours later, wet and frustrated. The rain had started again, coming down in a steady drizzle. His clothes were drenched, his hair plastered to his head. He sagged onto the sofa. "I couldn't find her anywhere. I went to all her friends' houses, my mom's house, Katie's house. My parents just got back from their cruise and my dad's out looking now, too. I went everywhere. I called George, the Lawford city police chief. The cops said they'd send a patrol car around." He ran a hand through his hair. "I can't find her."

Anita grabbed a towel and wrapped it around his shoulders. "She needs some time. She'll come around."

"What if she's run away for good?"

She shook her head. "I don't think so. Emily will be back. She's hurt right now, but she loves you."

His shoulders slumped. "I hope you're right."

She sat up and took him into her arms, intending to offer comfort, but knowing she was doing much more than that. Somewhere in the last few days, she'd gone beyond that.

"Luke." She wrapped him in a hug that blended the two of them into one, so tight she didn't quite know where she ended and he began.

"Oh, Anita. I need you right now." He dipped his head to her shoulder and held on tight, stroking his hand against her head. "Oh, God, Anita...I...I love you," he whispered.

She pulled back, her heart thumping wild and fast. "Luke, this...this is all moving too fast for me."

"Why?" His gaze sought hers. "Why are you so afraid of love?"

She sank back against the pillows and traced a finger along the plaid pattern of the sofa.

"Now who's being a turtle?"

A half smile crossed her lips. "You're right. I just don't talk about my past at all. With anyone."

"I'm not 'anyone.'"

She turned and looked at him, his gaze so clear and direct, so full of care and concern. And so much more. Had anyone ever looked at her that way in her life? "You're right."

"Then tell me."

A sigh escaped her. The thought of telling him, of talking about it all, suddenly didn't seem so bad anymore. He'd trusted her. Could she trust him? She connected again with his deep blue eyes, so familiar after all these years of friendship, and decided she could. "My mom died when I was ten. I wasn't lucky enough to have a dad around. I never even met my father. He didn't want anything to do with raising a kid, I guess, and my mom never talked about him. So, I went into foster homes. A lot of them. No one wanted a ten-year-old." She shrugged, as if it didn't really matter, but it had, and she could tell from his reaction that it must have shown on her face.

"Oh, honey," he said, bending down and stroking his hand along her cheek. His touch made it easier somehow to tell the story, to get the words past the lump in her throat, left there by years of disappointments.

"The older I got, the less I looked like that cute

little kid they could dress up, put in pigtails. I became a teenager. I rebelled a lot. Talked back. Failed classes. Not exactly anyone's dream child. They kept moving me from place to place.''

"How many foster homes were you in?"

"Seven. Eight." She shrugged again. "I lost count."

"I don't understand how the system can let that happen."

"It's better than an orphanage, I guess. When I was eighteen, I was on my own. I went to community college, got my degree, took care of myself. The best lesson I learned, though, was never get too attached."

"Because the families were so awful?"

"A lot of them weren't so bad. But whenever I liked one—" tears sprang up in her eyes "—well, that would be the one I'd have to leave, you know?" She swiped at her face. "Geez, I'm too old to get emotional about that."

He took her face in his hands, wiping away the tears with his thumbs. "So you came here, looking for home?"

"I...I guess I did. My mom always talked about how much she loved growing up in a small town, so I came to Mercy, kind of looking for the same thing."

"And did you find it?"

Had she? Had she finally found a place where she could put down roots? Wasn't that the one thing she'd always sought—and never found?

Because as much as she wanted it, the thought of staying in one place forever also terrified her.

A knock sounded at the door. Luke scrambled to

his feet and flung the door open. "Mr. Dole?" A
Lawford police officer stood on the other side. "I
think I've found your daughter."

"That was a complete waste of time." Luke let out
a chuff of disgust and sank onto Anita's porch. "I
don't know how that cop could have thought that girl
was my daughter. She didn't look anything at all like
Emily."

Anita rubbed his back. "Let's go inside, grab some
sandwiches and go back out and start looking for her
ourselves."

"You should be lying down and resting that knee."

"Not when you need me, Luke. There'll be plenty
of time for that later."

He captured her hand in his. "How'd I get so lucky
to meet you?"

She shook her head. "It wasn't luck."

"Come on, you don't believe in fate? Destiny?
Four-leaf clovers?"

She turned and walked up the porch steps. "Your
life is what you make it."

"Ah, I beg to differ." He got to his feet and followed her. "You moved here, to Mercy, out of all
the thousands of towns in the country. That was destiny."

She paused, her hand on the door handle and turned
to face him. "Maybe," she said, opening the door.

And then, there she was. After all they'd done and
gone through, the one thing they'd sought was already
home.

Emily sat on the couch, her knees tucked up under

her chin. She had a blanket wrapped around her and her hair hung in wet strands around her face. Luke rushed to her side. "Emily! Oh, Emily, where have you been?"

Anita stayed in the background, getting Emily a towel and then settling in a chair across from Luke, giving the two of them some privacy.

"I went back to that party." She sniffled. "I thought Kevin…I thought he'd be, like, nice to me because I was all upset. But…but he wasn't. He just wanted to party."

By the look in his eyes, Anita suspected Luke would gladly pummel Earring Boy into the pavement for being mean to his little girl.

"Those earrings probably make it hard for him to think straight," Luke said.

Emily gave him a watery smile. "That's a bad joke, Dad."

"Hey, I never said I was a comedian." His gaze connected with Anita's for a second. She'd heard the word *Dad*, too, and could see the relief in his eyes. All was not lost after all. Hope was an awfully powerful thing, Anita thought.

"I came back to talk to you and Anita." She produced a tissue from under the blanket and swiped at her nose. "I'm sorry for running away. I guess I was hurt. I thought about all of what you said while I was out there, just kinda walking in the rain and…I guess I understand."

"I never meant for you to find out that way, Em." Luke brushed a tear off her cheek. "I always meant to tell you. There just never seemed to be a good time.''

She nodded, then sniffled again. ''Do I have to go, like, live with other people?''

''No, baby.'' His voice was soft as a lullaby. ''You can stay with me. I'll always be your dad.''

She looked at him for a long second, her eyes watery pools. ''Is that why you always worked so much? 'Cause you didn't want to be with me?''

''Oh, Em,'' he drew her head to his chest, holding her tight to him. ''It was never that. *Never*. I always wanted you. I loved you so much. I just didn't know how to connect with you. They don't give you a book in the hospital, you know. And your mom, your mom was great. She made it too easy, I guess.''

Emily pulled back a little. ''Mom was cool, but...'' She swallowed, bit her lip. ''But I always felt closer to you somehow. Like, I don't know, like we were kinda the same. That sounds stupid now since we aren't even really related.''

Luke shook his head and Anita could hear his voice break. ''No, baby, it doesn't sound stupid at all. It's the sweetest thing I've ever heard.''

Emily nodded, then swallowed, as if she had a big lump in her throat. She paused, blew her nose, then sat up straighter. This time, she lowered her voice to a whisper. ''Are you, like, gonna marry Anita?''

''Would that be okay with you?''

Emily glanced over at Anita, chewed on her bottom lip. ''Yeah, she's cool. That'd be okay. Really okay.''

''Good.'' He cupped his daughter's face in his hands. ''You are the most important thing in the world to me. I'm going to try to be a better dad. Spend more time with you. Does that sound good?''

She nodded, then pressed the tissue to her eyes again. ''Yeah.''

''Great.'' He gave her a hug, then pulled back and wiped the damp strands of hair back from her face in a movement so tender, Anita could see every ounce of his love for his daughter in the simple gesture. ''Hey,'' he said with a grin, ''Anita made some cookies. How about the three of us go in the kitchen and start all over again?''

Emily nodded. ''That would be really great, Dad.''

After the cookies and a mug of decaf tea, Emily fell asleep on Anita's sofa. She curled up there like the little girl she still was, the blanket tucked around her, an angelic, peaceful look on her face.

Luke called everyone to tell them Emily was safe and then he and Anita settled in at the kitchen table, she with her legs propped up on a spare chair. She had some tea and some cookies but hadn't touched either. He sat across from her, toying with his mug.

''So, where do we go from here?'' he asked.

Anita looked at him. Did she dare? Luke had proven himself, not just with her, but with his daughter. He'd come out of his shell, opened his heart. Was there a possibility that fairy tales did come true? ''This hare is pretty tired of running.''

''Then let me take care of you for a while.'' He got up, came around the table and knelt beside her, taking both her hands in his. ''In case you forgot in the last hour or two, Anita, I love you.''

"Do you have any idea how scary it is for me to hear you say that?"

"Frankenstein scary or roller coaster scary?"

She laughed. "Roller coaster, I guess."

He released one of her hands and reached into his pocket. For a second, her breath caught. Then she saw what he held and she let out another laugh. "A very wise lady gave me this watch and told me to take chances once in a while. To live a lot and laugh often."

"I guess she needs to take that advice for herself, huh?"

"Yeah." He pressed the watch into her hand and closed her fingers over it. When he did, it set off the voice and Elmer sputtered, "Be vewy, vewy quiet. I'm hunting wabbits."

They both laughed then. A feeling of completeness washed over Anita as if she'd finally made the right choice. She wasn't rushing into anything with Luke. She'd known him for what felt like forever. He was a good man and he was no longer the workaholic she remembered. He was a committed man who would always put his family first. And he clearly wasn't going anywhere.

What more could she ask for?

She'd be crazy to let him get away.

"I hate it when you're right," she said, opening her palm and looking at the watch.

"Funny, because I love it when I am, and I think you should tell me I'm right on a daily basis."

"Hmm." She put a finger to her lips. "Guess that's

one of the things we'll have to compromise on then. Like whether we get a dog or a cat.''

He blinked. Twice. She could see the words processing in his head. ''Did you say—''

''Is your hearing going now? I said we'll have to learn to compromise if we're going to be together forever and ever. That is, if that proposal still stands.''

''What? Yes, it does. Yeah, of course.''

She grinned. ''I want to make sure of one thing, though.''

''What?''

She hesitated, flipping the watch face back and forth. ''Do you want to marry me because you love me or because you want to give another baby a father?''

In a second, he had scooped her up and into his arms. ''I'm marrying you because I love the way your hair flips over your shoulders. Because that red nail polish on your toes nearly makes me insane with wanting to kiss you. Because you're the first thing I think of when I wake up in the morning and the last thing I think of when I fall asleep. And because I love you so much, my heart feels like it's going to burst in two if you don't say yes this time.''

She smiled. ''Yes.'' Then she leaned forward and kissed him.

''Wait a minute.'' He pulled back. ''Why are *you* marrying *me?*''

''You have to ask?''

''I have to make sure it's not because I'm handy around the house.'' He glanced around the half-

finished kitchen. "I see you still need some maintenance done."

She gave his arm a good jab. "I'm marrying you
because I love you." She grinned. "The handyman
stuff is just a bonus."

"I knew there was a catch."

She smiled. "There always is. True happy endings
are only in fairy tales."

"Okay. I'll help you with this house, but we'll have
to work out a different payment schedule." The look
in his eyes was very, very devilish.

"Payment schedule?"

"Yeah." His voice had gone dark and sexy. "I
want half up front. *Now.*" He lowered his mouth to
hers and kissed her. Thoroughly and deeply.

Home, Anita realized, was right here, in Luke's
arms. It wasn't found in a small town or a rickety
rental house or even with a mouse. It was with the
man she loved. As long as she was with him, she was
home.

And that was a mighty fine place to be.

Epilogue

"Do you want Elmer?" Luke asked. He hovered by Anita's hospital bed, his eyes wide, dangling the watch in front of her.

At least he'd finally stopped pacing. Ever since she'd woken her husband up at three this morning to tell him labor had started, Luke had paced like a caged tiger.

"I don't need Elmer," she said. "He's no good as a focal point. Just hold my hand and help me breathe."

"You got it." He slipped his hand into hers and brought his face into her line of vision. His slow, even breathing helped Anita calm her racing heart and find a steady pace to deal with the waves of pain that came crashing over her in regular three-minute intervals. "Is that better?"

"Don't move and I'll be just fine."

He grinned. "Okay."

A commotion sounded outside the door and both Anita and Luke turned to look. Barbara and Steve were shuffling through the halls with Jan close beside them, calling out encouraging phrases. Barbara was clutching at her belly and moaning. "I want drugs. You promised me drugs. You didn't say anything about me having to walk around the hospital."

"Walking helps the baby come faster." Jan's voice was calm, patient.

"I'm not in a marathon, for God's sake," Barbara snapped. "Put me in a bed and get me an anesthesiologist."

Steve offered Jan an apologetic smile. "Soon, honey, soon," he told his wife.

"Don't 'honey' me. You're the reason I'm in this mess. If you think I'm changing a single diaper after I have your child, think again, buddy. Get the wipes ready, because payback is coming." She shuffled away.

Luke glanced at Anita. When their eyes met, they both burst out laughing. "Payback, huh?" he said.

"Oh, I got plenty of that—" Anita paused to huff and puff through a contraction "—planned for you."

Luke brushed a tendril of hair off her forehead. "I can hardly wait." He leaned down and placed a soft, tender kiss on her lips.

"What was that for?"

"For being my wife. For being the most incredible thing that's ever happened to me. For giving me back my daughter."

She smiled. "I think you did that one on your own." She closed her eyes as another contraction came right on top of the last one. When it finally passed, she took in a breath. "Stick with me, Luke, and I think I'll be giving you a son, too."

"I'm not going anywhere, Anita." He held both of her hands tight in his, forgetting the watch in his palm. "Ever."

A muffled Elmer sputtered something about hunting wabbits but neither of them heard him. They were too busy completing their family.

* * * * *

If you enjoyed what you just read,
then we've got an offer you can't resist!

Take 2 bestselling love stories FREE!

Plus get a FREE surprise gift!

Clip this page and mail it to Silhouette Reader Service

IN U.S.A.	IN CANADA
3010 Walden Ave.	P.O. Box 609
P.O. Box 1867	Fort Erie, Ontario
Buffalo, N.Y. 14240-1867	L2A 5X3

YES! Please send me 2 free Silhouette Romance® novels and my free surprise gift. After receiving them, if I don't wish to receive anymore, I can return the shipping statement marked cancel. If I don't cancel, I will receive 6 brand-new novels every month, before they're available in stores! In the U.S.A., bill me at the bargain price of $21.34 per shipment plus 25¢ shipping and handling per book and applicable sales tax, if any*. In Canada, bill me at the bargain price of $24.68 plus 25¢ shipping and handling per book and applicable taxes**. That's the complete price and a savings of at least 10% off the cover prices—what a great deal! I understand that accepting the 2 free books and gift places me under no obligation ever to buy any books. I can always return a shipment and cancel at any time. Even if I never buy another book from Silhouette, the 2 free books and gift are mine to keep forever.

209 SDN DU9H
309 SDN DU9J

Name	(PLEASE PRINT)	
Address	Apt.#	
City	State/Prov.	Zip/Postal Code

* Terms and prices subject to change without notice. Sales tax applicable in N.Y.
** Canadian residents will be charged applicable provincial taxes and GST.
   All orders subject to approval. Offer limited to one per household and not valid to
   current Silhouette Romance® subscribers.
   ® are registered trademarks of Harlequin Books S.A., used under license.

SROM03   ©1998 Harlequin Enterprises Limited

LUNA

On wings of fire she rises...

Born without caste or position in Arukan, a country that
prizes both, Kevla Bai-sha's life is about to change. Her
feverish dreams reveal looming threats to her homeland
and visions of the dragons that once watched over her
people—and held the promise of truth. Now, Kevla,
together with the rebel prince of the ruling household,
must sacrifice everything and defy all law and tradition,
to embark on a daring quest to save the world.

On sale June 29.
Visit your local bookseller.

SILHOUETTE *Romance*

COMING NEXT MONTH

#1726 HER SECOND-CHANCE MAN—Cara Colter
High school outsider Jessica Moran could never forget golden
boy Brian Kemp's teasing smile—or the unlikely friendship
they'd shared when she'd helped him heal a sick dog. So
when Brian walked back into her life fourteen years later,
with another sick puppy and a rebellious teenager in tow, Jessica knew she was being given a second chance at love....

#1727 CINDERELLA'S SWEET-TALKING MARINE—
Cathie Linz
Men of Honor
Captain Ben Kozlowski was a marine with a mission!
Sworn to protect the sister of a fallen soldier, he marched into
Ellie Jensen's life and started issuing orders. But this sassy
single mother had some rules of her own, and before long,
Ben found himself wanting to promise to love and honor
more than to serve and protect.

#1728 CALLIE'S COWBOY—Madeline Baker
When Native American rancher Cade Kills Thunder came to
her rescue on a remote Montana highway, Callie Walker was
in heaven. The man was even more handsome than the male
models that graced the covers of her romance novels! Would
Callie be able to capture this rugged rancher's attention...and
his heart?

#1729 THE BOSS'S BABY SURPRISE—Lilian Darcy
Soulmates
Cecilia Rankin kept having the weirdest dreams, like visions
of her sexy boss, Nick Delaney, soothing a crying child.
But when her dream began to come true and Nick ended up
guardian of his sister's baby, Celie knew that Nick really *was*
the man of her dreams.

SRCNM0604